Justin

The Boy in the Skull Mask

Editions Dedicaces

THE BOY IN THE SKULL MASK

Published by:
    Editions Dedicaces LLC
    12759 NE Whitaker Way, Suite D833
    Portland, Oregon, 97230
    www.dedicaces.us

Library of Congress Cataloging-in-Publication Data
    Wilson, Justin
      The Boy in the Skull Mask /
      by Justin Wilson.
      p. cm.
      ISBN-13: 978-1-77076-419-4 (alk. paper)
      ISBN-10: 1-77076-419-4 (alk. paper)

Justin Wilson

The Boy in the Skull Mask

Prologue

The resounding clap of thunder that echoed through streets was enough to rattle the smaller buildings in the area. Every creature with senses, that lived within radius of the sound, either reacted—dogs barking, cat hissing while trying to find refuge from the pouring rain—or simply ignored it in favor continuing their nightly routines. In one of the houses, a couple that had likely been married for some years were fighting over some mundane issue. On the other side of town, there was likely a newlywed couple enjoying the rewards of each other's bodies at the exact same moment. But the man currently going about his business couldn't be bothered by the thunder.

He was too busy making his usual rounds on patrol, searching the abandoned residences for anything out of the ordinary. Old rundown places like these were host to a number of things: murder, rape, satanic rituals involving sacrifices, and, his personal favorite, séances. People who thought they could talk to the spirits of loved ones using witchcraft, voodoo, and Ouija boards. He still couldn't believe people *actually* thought those damn things worked. Especially when you could probably order one on Amazon or eBay. But that was the average person for you, always willing to spend money on stuff that only "worked" on the word of some sales rep.

Of course, it didn't help that he lived in New Orleans, Louisiana, where this nonsense has some supposed base. That pretty much meant he dealt with all of things, but in spades.

Just six more months, he thought with resigned determination. *Six more months, then this'll be someone else's job to deal with this crazy shit every night.* In six more months, he'd be retired and headed for Dallas to live out the rest of his days on his brother's ranch. This time next spring, he'll be growing crops, hatching chickens, and milking cows. He'll work all day and sleep all night—instead of the other way around. He'd met some nice little cowgirl and get married, teach his son how to play basketball and walk his daughter down the aisle on her wedding day.

That was it. Nothing too big or small, just a nice little quiet life under the Texas sun rather than a Louisiana monsoon in the middle of October. With Halloween just around the corner, it only made things worse where he was concerned. Every nut job who claimed to be an advocate for Satan would be out gutting goats and drinking their blood. Teens would go around pissing in cemeteries on some ridiculous dare to rile the spirits. And every psycho not locked up would stalk some poor soul and leave their body to rot in one these buildings he was currently searching.

He didn't mean for the thought to sound so cynical but that was the world he and everyone else lived in. People killing each other for things like money, women, or just for the thrill. He knew he would eventually find some unfortunate Joe or Jane who happen to be in the wrong place at the wrong time. And it would only get a mention in the news if the person was killed in some spectacular way. Glorify the killer and give them a following of people who'll eventually do the same thing.

And the next day, people would just forget, probably be a little more cautious and lock their doors if the killer wasn't found soon. But they'd forget nonetheless.

When the hell did we all become so damn complacent?

He blamed a myriad of things: television, Facebook, YouTube, etc. Crap like that is why the each new generation comes out worst than the last. They think the whole world is going to bow down and kiss their ass. Made him think of a time when he found to teens having sex in one the old bars. They'd cursed at him—the girl tossed a brick at him, just barely missing—and ran off. The next day, he'd gone to the gas station to get his car washed and found the other teen from that night worked there.

The little punk actually looked like he was gonna piss his pants the moment he saw and he'd managed to get a free tank out the deal for not ratting him out to his boss about the incident. He'd be lying if he said he didn't smile the rest of the day like he was on some kind of high. The thought still brought a small grin to his lips every now and then. He taught that kid lesson about humility and made damn sure he'd respect his elders. He shook his head, "Look at me. Talking about how *they're* the ones who need to stop being arrogant."

6

That's when he heard it.

A sound, loud enough to be heard over the rain and thunder, and coming from the alley. He sighed, a puff of steam flowing from his lips and nose. It was *always* an alley. Readying his hand to grab the gun that rested on his waist belt, he slowly, carefully, entered the alley. He thought back to the sound, what it could be. It was a loud *thud*, so odds are it was a dead body being dumped somewhere.

Whoever they were, they picked a perfect night to kill somebody; the rain was probably washing away all the evidence anyway so moving the body wouldn't really matter. But it seems like this guy thought it was better to be safe than sorry. That meant there was likely a serial killer about to grace their fines streets with his evil. Just great, he thought bitterly, that all we need around here, some whacko trying to be the next big name in news. Those idiots would probably give him some stupid name like "The Rainy Day Killer" or "Pouring Prowler".

He hugged the wall just in case lightning flashed; he didn't want to alert the killer if they were still here. He reached the corned and sucked in a deep breath of air to ease his rapidly beating heart. He may have grown used to these kinds of situations but that didn't meant they didn't still scare him. Every time he did something like this he risked getting bullet to the head or a knife across his throat. But he owed it to the poor victim and their family to at least make sure they were given a proper funeral. He waited one more minute before pulling his gun from its holster and rounding the corner.

"Freeze!"

The alley appeared to be empty as he moved in deeper, careful not to create too much noise and was mindful of any splashing his boots might make. Swallowing nervously, he slowly scanned the area with his light. He was careful not to miss anything of importance (not that there was) and record it for memory. Every detail would be needed for the report if this turned out to be some kind of murder. But it couldn't be a murder without a body.

He was starting to think his mind was playing tricks on him until he stepped in something that didn't feel like it belonged in an alley. Looking down, he saw what he could only guess was ash. There were plenty of chimneys around here so it wasn't out of the ordinary but it just seemed odd for ash to show up in an alley of all places. It did not escape him that there was a distinct possibility that this ash might have been a person once. If it was, he would say a prayer for them later and ask their forgiveness. He still wondered if the ash had anything to do with the *thud*.

But how could ash hitting the ground make a noise loud enough to hear over thunder and rain?

This was starting to get a bit more interesting and dreadful at the same time. Checking the alley one more time, he found nothing to suggest that a murder had taken place. Of course, there was always the possibility that the murderer moved the body inside for some reason. And that meant having to look in all the buildings again. He checked the ground for any signs of blood (not that he would find any in the rain).

That's when he heard what, most definitely, was a gunshot.

Well shit, he thought when he his heart stopped racing, now that changes things. He was most definitely risking a bullet to the head if he ventured further but he couldn't stop now. If there was no body, it meant the would-be victim was probably alive. He thought for a moment before realizing just where the gunshot had come from. The roof of the old bar antique shop of all places. Was this some kind of gang-style execution?

Finding the old ladder, he places the flashlight between his teeth and started climbing, just as another gunshot was heard. He nearly fell but kept on going. If he had to guess, these shots were probably meant to be confused for thunder. Definitely sounds like this was planned out, he pondered, so what's there to be gained? When he finally reached the top, he got his answer.

And boy, did he, for once, wish it was just some teens having sex.

He was so shocked by what he saw that his mouth dropped open and flashlight fell to the ground. The drop was enough to break it and leave him in the dark to watch the shadow puppetry of what was going on before him.

There stood two figures on either side of the building, both of them male from the proportions of their bodies. But they were not starting each other down, but rather something that looked like it was dreamt up by some kid hopped up on acid. Thankfully for him, it was only in the shadows as he probably would crapped himself if he saw what that thing was supposed to look like in proper lighting.

Standing on all fours, the silhouette of the monster had what appeared to be jagged spikes protruding from its shoulder, spine, and—was that a tail? The shape seemed to be rippling with his muscle and its head appeared to akin to a lions. That was really the best he could come up with as it moved with inhuman speed toward one of the two men on the right. Before he could call out to either of them (and say what exactly?), the figure it had targeted moved to meet the beast head on. Rather than use physical force, he revealed a blade that gleamed like pale blue moonlight.

He managed to avoid being struck by the beast before it moved toward his partner, unleashing a shriek that could almost shatter glass. But he too was prepared, perhaps even *better* some might say. He aimed his gun at the monster and fired—the gunshot that he must have heard that brought him up here in the first place. The monster cried out in pain before the guy with the sword leaped into the air and brought the tip of the blade down through the beast's head. It thrashed about for a few minutes before giving up and dying.

A few moments later, the beast disappeared into what he assumed was ash, the same kind he stepped in down there. So there were more of those things? If so, how many? And what were they to begin with?

His thoughts were put on hold when he realized to the figures were staring him. Before he could react, lightning streaked across the sky, illuminating everything below it. And in that instance, he saw the eyes of one of the figures. A cold pale sliver gaze, as though it were steel, regarded him with a stern expression. He was so startled that he pulled back on instinct, slipping off the ladder and down to the alley below.

The back of his head slammed against the dumpster and blood began pouring out of his skull as he lay there, almost sure he was dying. He closed his eyes, the last thought in his head,, not of the ranch, the family, the peace that denied him, but of what he had just seen. The monster, the ash, and more importantly, the silver-eyed man with the sword.

Chapter 1

The flies had begun to swarm thickly. The body had been found at high noon, by some street skaters using the alleys for a shortcut. Only one of them bothered to stick around so as to answer any questions, leading to the speculation that one or more of them had a record. Probably something relating to dead bodies, if one was to make an educated guess. Still, they called the police rather than simply leave the body to decompose in the daylight, so it had to count for something. But that would only provide little comfort to the victim or his family.

Detective Renee Chavez had just arrived at the scene, pushing hurriedly through the crowd that had gathered at the edge of the alley. She was not looking forward to examining a body that was already becoming a feast for the insects. She hated insects with passion ever since a wasp stung her in the shoulder when she was only five, forcing her mother to use a small knife to cut out the stinger. She cried for a good hour after that. Her father immediately called the exterminator and had them dealt with. But her dislike of insects remained until it morphed into a flat out hatred.

Flies were no wasps (that much was obvious) but she like any normal person hated that buzzing in her ears.

Ducking under police tape, she rounded the corner to find that the crime scene had already been set up. Off to the side, the lone skater was answering questions about how he and his friends had found the body. The kid looked harmless enough to rule him out as a suspect. That and his obvious trepidation at approaching a body suggested he was too squeamish to even crush a bug under his shoe. She diverted her attention back to the matter at hand as she approached the body.

Clad in a beat cop uniform and a poncho to keep the rain at bay, carrying a nothing but a gun and what remained of a broken flashlight, the dark skin on his body had paled into a graying complexion. His light brown eyes were dull, the flame of life that had likely burned brightly in him once before had been forever dimmed. His gaze stared straight up at the sky and she at least hoped he'd seen something worthwhile before he passed on. With a sigh, Chavez slipped on her latex gloves and searched him for an ID.

The flies buzzed angrily at having the eventual home for their larva disturbed but their inconvenience was of no bother to her.

Pulling out his wallet she learned that his name was Simon C. Ribe.

"Good afternoon to you, Officer Ribe," she greeted. "I'm sorry we had to meet under these circumstances. From the looks of things, you were just doing your job before someone decided it was reason enough to kill you. Or maybe you just didn't like your work and threw away your life. Either way, I'm not here to judge."

"You always gotta talk to the stiffs, Chavez?" asked her partner, Jackson Hyde. Having just finished taking statements from the skater kid, he moved to join her. "No wonder people think all you Cajuns are voodoo priests."

"You get anything from the kid?" she asked in lieu of responding to his jab.

"Says they were riding through when they found the body. He decided to stick around when his friends bailed. Doesn't think they had anything to do with it though. But he also admits he doesn't know them well enough to be sure. But back to your suggestion, you think he jumped?"

"I don't see anything resembling a gun shot or a knife wound on him, do you? Who knows, he might have been pushed or just fell off the ladder because it was slippery that night."

"Guess we'll let the doc figure it out, huh?"

They hadn't been partners long enough to socialize outside of work but they were together long enough to form a rapport. Hyde was still nonplussed by her tendency to speak with the dead, promising to give them some kind of closure. Chavez simply played straight man (*woman*, as he would constantly remind her) to his jovial jabs. Her patience is probably why the captain had decided to pair them up.

Of course there was also a rumor about him from before he transferred here from Boston—he'd never said where he was from, but his accent gave it away. They were naturally suspicious of each other at first, particularly because Chavez had mentioned it was a rather long way to travel for simple transfer. Whatever Hyde had done at his last job must have pissed off a lot of people. But she found that she could trust him to an extent. That was enough for now.

***

Dr. Grace Marshall had been chief medical examiner for the last five years and Chavez knew enough to know when she was in a foul mood. While she was by no means a warm woman on any regular occasion, considering most of their interactions involved dealing with the dead, there were days when her business-like demeanor was turned up to near robotic nature.

Today was one of those days.

Hyde could only guess it had something to do with her latest trial, having to deal with a defense attorney who didn't even bother to question her credibility as a forensic pathologist simply because she was an African-American woman. While she couldn't care less in the court room, he'd apparently said something that one didn't normally say in a civilized conversation. It certainly didn't help that he was the only white guy in the room right now.

She'd just finished cleaning up at the autopsy when they entered the room, the sweet and sour stench of death still hanging in the air. Dressed in her pale green scrubs that emphasized her dark skin complexion, she regarded them both with a steely dark gaze behind thinly framed glasses. Her black hair cropped just above the nape of her neck. Her voice carried the slightest tinge of a Creole accent.

"The gash on the back of his head was, as I'm sure you've both surmised, the result of him hitting the dumpster below. The impact of the wound suggests he fell from a great distance, either from the top of the building or the ladder. He likely died on impact."

"Can you tell us if he was pushed?" asked Chavez.

"It's extremely rare for anyone to choose jumping off a building as a form of suicide, unless they want to be seen. For some people, it's all about the 'spectacle' detective. Jumping off a building in the middle of a storming night, while unique, makes no sense. Not to mention he landed on the *back* of his head and hit the dumpster. None of it lines up with suicide."

"Could he have been climbing up the ladder to jump off the building when he just slipped?" Hyde inquired. Dr. Marshall set her laser-like gaze on him for a moment before returning her attention to her charts.

"Possible," she admitted, "but the way he was dressed suggests he took his job seriously or at least was resigned to work as diligently as possible before his retirement."

"So what's the call, doc?" Chavez crossed her arms. "Did you find any signs of foul play or did our friend here jump?"

Marshall sighed and looked up from the charts, "It's impossible to tell. Given that he was left out in the rain all night, any evidence that might have suggested murder has likely been washed away. I can't tell you the number of times a suicide turned out to be a homicide."

Chavez and Hyde exchanged glances and sighed; it was clear that further investigation was required. They would have to speak with everyone who knew Ribe well enough to tell if he was suicidal or not. Marshall seemed apologetic for her expressing her doubts but Chavez reassured her with a hesitant smile. The last thing she needed was to feed the doubt planted in her mind by some bigot in a suit that was bought and paid for by exonerating guilty men. She looked to Hyde, "Let's talk to everyone who knew him and see if he showed any signs of depression."

"There's one other thing," Marshall flipped through her chart. "CSI found what appeared to be ash on the bottom of his boots. Considering they couldn't find anything else like it at the crime scene or the roof, it's rather odd."

Hyde looked intrigued. There hadn't been anything remotely resembling ash in the area, though there were plenty of chimneys and it had been real cold last night. He wouldn't be surprised if there were dumpsters filled with plastic bags of ash. But the fact that it hadn't dissolved under the heavy rain was telling.

Chavez nodded, "See if you can find anything that'll lead us to a potential suspect. If he was murdered, who did he piss off or what did he see?"

***

They'd searched Ribe's home—a small structure akin to a hut, according to Hyde—before checking with neighbors to learn about their victim's personal life. From what they had gathered, although Simon C. Ribe had no significant other or close friends, he was a nice guy and they couldn't imagine anyone wanting to hurt him. The prospect of suicide also drew disbelief as Ribe was apparently Baptist. Still, it wouldn't be the first time a man of religious faith took his own life.

Hyde had suggested to his neighbors that Ribe might have been Gay—which brought up the possibility that it had not been suicide but rather that he fell victim to some bigoted colleague who believed Ribe was committing some form of blasphemy—but they had vehemently denied the allegation.

Chavez thought on it for a moment though. Although being openly gay was more widely accepted by the public now than it had been years earlier, bigotry and discrimination were still prevalent. Add to the fact that Ribe was African-American, and it would only make matters worse. But there were plenty of single women they had spoken to who attested that Ribe was undoubtedly attracted to the opposite sex. It didn't matter to Chavez if it was true or not; gay or straight, she would seek justice for Simon C. Ribe regardless.

Their next stop was the local church.

News of Ribe's death had inspired a wake to be held once the body was released—the brother was to arrive later in the week. People were already gathering to offer their prayers for his soul to find eternal rest. The two detectives went around back and knocked on the door to the mess hall. A woman answered and they flashed their badges and asked to speak with whomever was in charge. She seemed hesitant to let them in, but a hand on her shoulder assured her it was fine.

"Good afternoon, detectives," the man to whom the hand belonged to, greeted them. The door opened to reveal a man dressed in the attire of a reverend. Gentle green eyes beneath sand colored hair smiled at them the way a person would smile at two kids who seemed overly curious. "I am Michael Strauss. I assume you're here to inquire about Simon."

"If it's not too much trouble, Reverend," Chavez and Hyde stepped through the door into the church. She didn't like the feeling of carrying her gun into what was considered to be a holy sanctuary. Nor did she like the idea of shooting someone if need be. Those were just the kind of thoughts one had when entering the house of God.

Strauss led them into his office, asking his secretary to step out for a moment so that he could speak with the detectives in private. She eyed them somewhat warily, but complied nonetheless. He took a seat and offered them the two chairs in front of his desk. He sighed:

"We were all quite shocked when the news broke. Simon was beloved by everyone and did his part to keep the streets safe at night. Such a shame."

"Were you aware that he was planning on retiring in six months?" Hyde asked, taking out a notepad.

"I was, he announced it to the congregation this past Wednesday. We were planning on throwing him a going away party, the day he retired."

"I know you said he was 'beloved' by everyone, but it's hard to imagine a beat cop not having some enemies, wouldn't you agree?"

"I'm aware that police work is not the safest, nor the most popular, job out there, but I'm afraid there's no one here, that I'm aware of, that harbored any malice towards Simon. If I sensed something was wrong, I would have done my best to speak with them."

Chavez didn't want to be the one to ask this, but it had to be done. "What if the problem was a disagreement over life choices?"

Strauss caught on quickly, "Detective, I assure you that among my duties, I find it most important to spread the message of tolerance and acceptance, no matter someone's personal orientations. Though I think you are mistaken in this case. Simon was at times popular with the ladies. He didn't date a lot, but he was a gentlemen."

Chavez nodded and watched as Hyde jotted down more notes when a knock from behind interrupted them. The secretary poked her head inside and gestured outside (clearly not wanting to discuss this in front of two cops). Strauss nodded and asked for a brief moment before following her. She sighed and took in the office while Hyde finished jotting down what he'd just learned.

A moment later, Strauss returned, "I'm terribly sorry detectives, but something has come up. A friend is in need of some advice on how to deal with Simon's death. They were apparently close. I'll be glad to finish answering you're questions tomorrow."

"That's okay," Hyde said. "You pretty much answered all of them. We'll get out of your hair now."

Chavez handed the Reverend her card and the two detectives exited the church and Hyde took out his cell phone. Before Chavez could ask, he started texting. Judging from what it appeared to be, he was texting someone not involved in the case. She decided that she might as well tease him a bit.

"Hot date?"

"Something like that?"

"What are they like?"

"Athletic, likes to sit in and watch movies, enjoys the occasional dinner."

"You serious?"

"Getting there."

"Got a name.

"Martin."

Chavez stood there dumbstruck, she knew enough about her partner to know he wouldn't joke about this. That meant Jackson Hyde was gay and had just witnessed her asking a rather inappropriate question with him right next to her. She could feel her cheeks flare up in embarrassment as they got in the car.

"Hyde—"

"Don't sweat it, the only reason I didn't tell you, or the precinct, is because none of you asked. Not really anyone else's business you know?"

"That's fair."

Hyde smirked and started up the car and they drove off. Awkwardness aside; they still had a killer to catch.

Chapter 2

Thom Braddock stood outside of the elevator that led from the garage to the halls of the precinct when Chavez and Hyde returned after a day's work of investigating the death of Simon C. Ribe. Braddock had been the captain of the New Orleans Police Department Homicide Division Unit for nearly fifteen years. Hyde noted whereas Chavez was a Latina woman with short black hair that stopped at her neck and light brown eyes, Braddock was an African-American man with graying stubble on his scalp, dark eyes watching them as they joined him in the elevator. Arms crossed over a broad chest, white shirt covering a strong physique, he looked every bit the veteran he was. He nodded at them both and leaned against the wall of the small box carrying them.

The entire precinct shifted about in an orderly fashion when the doors opened up, but Chavez caught the whispers of gossip. Normally, when a fellow officer died, the entire department would be out hunting his killer. But it seemed there was no one willing to avenge Ribe's death—Chavez didn't hadn't come across anyone who'd known him terribly well—or even admit there was someone to be blamed. Did that mean everyone just accepted the idea that he'd taken his own life? Whatever the reason, something about all this was off.

"I'm sure I don't need to tell the both of you that we've got more important cases to work on than looking into what appears to be a suicide," Braddock said as he marched through halls to the squad room. "But since the coroner doesn't seem willing to label it one or the other, enlighten me on your progress."

"So far, it looks like Ribe had no one who disliked him enough to throw him off a rooftop," Chavez began.

"And no one seems willing to believe he'd just up and take his own life, either," Hyde added.

Braddock paused for a moment, eyes closed and stroking his chin thoughtfully, as though he were in a meditative state. He quickly reopened his eyes and started toward his office again, "Anything to suggest it was just an accident?"

"Seems like the only plausible explanation," she replied.

Crossing the squad room floor, they entered the captain's office, decorated with award and accommodations for his years of service, and a window shining the light of the afternoon sun; his desk was lined with photos of his days in uniform, newspaper articles concerning arrests he'd made, and a picture of his son. There was a pretty solemn story there, according to the rumor mill, but neither Chavez nor Hyde would comment on it. Braddock took seat and invited them to do the same. For a moment, he sat there, studying them, gauging how well their partnership was going, and making sure they were on the same page.

He then changed the subject, "There were reports of a pretty gruesome scene down at the old theatre. Seems like Alex Roan is sending a message to his competition."

At the mention of Alex Roan's name, Chavez scowled deeply, a familiar anger bubbling in her stomach.

She flipped on the lights in her apartment and locked the door, relaxing after another grueling day of undercover work for Narcotics. Working as one of Roan's girls had its perks, that much was certain. She wasn't sure how she'd leave this deluxe apartment to go back to her average home in the suburbs. But at least there was someone waiting for her when she got back.

I guess marriage has its own "perks", Renee Kaplan thought with a rueful smile.

She felt bad for leaving her husband, Ricardo—or "Ricky" as their friends called him—alone when he'd just gotten back from a month long stay at an oiling rig in Texas. But they both had their jobs to do and she had gotten farther than any other officer in her unit. Everyone had a blind spot, be they man or woman. The case being that Roan's blind spot was a woman. *She didn't like to think how his eyes roaming over made her skin crawl. The feeling was unusual; she'd only ever felt this way when around bugs.*

Whatever it was, the sooner she gathered the evidence necessary to link him to the drug trade, the sooner she'd be rid of this uneasy feeling. Not many of the detectives sent undercover had gotten as far as she did. She ignored the whispers among the unit that it was because she had "something" they lacked. She knew how to go the extra mile when the situation demanded it. A guy like Alex Roan was too busy stripping every woman he saw with his eyes to notice things and she played that to her advantage.

She'd barely had time to put her bags down when someone crashed through her door. She spun on her heel just in time to catch a glimpse of Alex Roan just before his goon cracked something hard and blunt over her skull.

Alex Roan was currently considered the kingpin of crime in New Orleans, his criminal organizations spread across the eight districts covered by NOPD. One of their shrinks figured this design was born of the belief that order and chaos were two sides of the same coin. Whatever the reason, Roan had a hand in just about every major dealing that went on in the city. If there was something of value to be traded or bought illegally, he'd be there with a blank check. His dubious reputation, however, didn't stop him from being a regular on the social circuit. His night club, *Bête Noir,* was frequented by many of NOLA's movers and shakers, none of them caring that he was criminal who'd gut them just as soon as serve them champagne. But he always manage to say ahead of law enforcement, which only served to boost his massive ego.

"Who was stupid enough to muscle in on Roan's turf now?" Hyde asked.

"They don't have a name as far as I can tell, probably because he wiped 'em all out before they could even come up with one," Braddock leaned back. "I figure the two of you might as well head down there since nothing seems to be forming from the Ribe case. It probably won't turn into anything useful, but we've got an oath to uphold."

***

The old theatre had been abandoned ever since Katrina, the water damage leaving the building structurally unsound. A new one was built during the recovery effort and played home to many successful performances since. But that didn't stop any sort of illegal activity from taking place in the old building. It was just the kind of place a roach like Alex Roan would scamper off to find protection from the light. Chavez made sure her gun was loaded and her spare was within reach before getting out of the car.

Despite Hyde being there to back her up, she couldn't help feeling entirely alone whenever it came cases dealing with Roan. It trudged up too many unpleasant memories.

She was so consumed by her thoughts, she didn't notice the vibration of her smart phone in her pocket. They entered the building together, C.S.I. following them in once they made sure it was safe. The passage had been narrowed by debris. The ground crunched beneath their feet and it smelled of water and mold that had likely been here for a while—most likely since Katrina, making it the perfect place to leave a rotting corpse.

Except someone had screwed up.

She wondered briefly what Alex Roan would have thought if one of his goons had left evidence linking him to whatever awaited them inside this old deathtrap. Roan prided himself on being five moves ahead in the chess game he played with the police. He thought of everything that could go wrong with his plans; of anything the police would try to get him to slip up (undercover officers, stakeouts, raids, etc.). The idea that there was something capable of throwing a wrench into his plans was too good to be true.

Still, Chavez held back a grin at the thought of seeing his face twisted in his surprise; some fantasies were better left to one's self.

They finally reached the end of the narrow passageway and stepped up their pace. The deeper they ventured, the higher the risk was that they'd end up trapped in here if something were to happen. When they emerged, what they were greeted with forced Renee to think back to what Captain Braddock said: that this was a gruesome sight.

That didn't even begin to describe it.

It was a goddamned massacre.

Chapter 3

Detective Chavez noted that the first that always seemed to stick out in any crime scene she'd investigated, was the blood. It lent to the belief some killers clung to: that they were artists. The world was their canvas, and the human body was an endless supply of paint with which to convey their world's image. Anyone of the same mindset was sure to have been pleased with the sight Chavez and Hyde came upon in the old theatre. Lucky for them, they weren't, otherwise she would shot them dead with her gun.

Whoever had done this took the time to leave behind florescent lights provided an eerie glow that reminded her of moonlight. The theatre had been stripped of anything useful so that its successor could be made as cheaply as possible. Rows of chairs stood bare of the red cushions and golden arm rests. Only the metal skeletons had been left bolted to the floors, an amber-colored rust setting in.

Curtains hung parted in dust-filled tatters, the stage floor reflecting the eerie glow of the light in an ethereal display. Like any canvas, all anyone took notice of was the "artwork", notably the blood that glowed in the room's lighting. And it had a gruesome story for their eyes only.

Strung up above the stage like a puppet was—what Chavez and Hyde assumed—was one of the victims. Something thin and razor sharp spread his arms apart, cutting through his wrists to the bone, while suspending him in the air as though he were frozen. He'd been stripped naked, blood running down to pool below his feet. The conditions of the room only seemed to speed up the decomposition, his skin already a sickly gray color, flies buzzing around eagerly. Behind him, his companion sat upright against the wall in the back, head tilted as if questioning them on why it had taken so long for someone to notice them. Torn clothes were stained red while promising a dark tale of their own. One more sat in the front row, head gazing up at the sky much like Simon Ribe had been this morning.

Chavez guessed he had been forced to watch the gruesome slaughter of their friends, if the ropes tied around the body were anything to go on. The blood splatter at the edge of the stage suggested he'd been the last to go, torso ripped open.

Even for the two detectives, who'd seen their fair share of brutality—individually and collectively—this seemed a little much. Alex Roan was no saint (Chavez was sure her religious mother would grab her crucifix and start muttering a prayer if he was ever near her), that much was clear. But this seemed a little too . . . primal for him; he prided himself on his gentlemen's conduct. But something had convinced the captain he was involved, so the task of finding that connection was left to her and Hyde. Gathering herself, fighting the bile rising in her throat, Chavez turned to the C.S.I. team.

They were having their own troubles keeping the shock and utter disgust from showing on their faces. You could only treat scenes like these with clinical disinterest for so long. She waited for them to tame their instincts to run and hide before speaking. "Okay, let's start canvasing the scene."

They seemed grateful for the distraction of work.

"What do you make of this, Hyde?"

He shook his head, "I don't know. I get that Roan's sending a message, but *this*... It's just going too far. I can probably guess the guy tied to the chair was in charge. The killer made him watch while he gutted his people. I can think of a few reasons why someone would do this; retaliation, some kind of sick occult ritual, or our main theory; Alex Roan sending a message.

Message received, Hyde thought grimly. *Stay out of my turf.*

When the forensic teams were done setting up the scene, Chavez and Hyde pulled on their latex gloves and the search for anything useful. Hyde was reminded of that scene from an old horror movie he'd seen. One where the cops investigating the case didn't make it out alive.

Then a sound caught his attention.

A frightened shape tried to make a run for it, but Chavez caught it, holding on tightly; then the shape started screaming. Turning his full attention on them, he saw it was some girl, and his heart sank. It was bad enough knowing Roan had made the stiff in the front row watch this butchering, but a girl, who looked no

24

older than twenty-one, knowing that just made him sick. Brown, curly, hair covered wide, haunted eyes, the desire to avoid whatever fate had befallen these three men burning brightly. Her arms and legs were long and athletic, she could hold her own in fight. Her tan skin reminded Hyde of caramel, although it was paler from the shock.

She finally stopped squirming and settled down, mumbling something in Spanish.

"You're okay," Chavez comforted in the same tongue, "it's going to be all right. I'm Detective Chavez, this," she gestured to Hyde "is Detective Hyde. We're with the police. Can you tell us what happened? Who did this?"

The girl only said one audible word"

"*El Diablo.*"

Chapter 4

"*El Diablo?*" Captain Braddock repeated incredulously. Having just arrived in time to see the young girl carted off into an ambulance bound for Oschner. She had continuously repeated the same thing over and over again, insisting that what had killed her friends was *El Diablo:* The Devil. Chavez and Hyde weren't able get anything more out of her, so they called for an ambulance. Maybe the doctors could help her make sense of what she witnessed.

The sky painted a mural the colors of orange and purple, the sun just setting beyond the horizon. The light reflected off the buildings, suggesting a beauty to this world greater than what lay inside the old theatre at the moment. After C.S.I. finished its canvas of the scene, orderlies from the Office of the Coroner arrived and started loading the remains into the truck for delivery to the morgue.

"That's all she said," Hyde answered. "We couldn't get her to elaborate. She's pretty shaken up, Captain."

"If she wasn't, then I'd be quick to label her a suspect. How do we know she isn't faking the shock? Appearing to survive a brutal slaying like this would pretty much guarantee all eyes searching in every other direction." Braddock was reminded of a case he'd worked as a detective. College girl claimed her professor raped her. He'd it was consensual; that she liked it rough, the usual bit. His lawyer argued that her major in theatre arts called into question her credibility.

Eventually, the jury voted him guilty and he was given the maximum sentence. But his trial had added another layer of scrutiny that victims had to endure to seek justice. Braddock shook away the memory and focused on the here and now. There was a killer out there who needed to be caught and who might be in some way connected to Alex Roan. If they could nail him for this...

He cleared his throat, "I want you two to find out every-thing you can about this. Who these guys are, what their connection—if any—to Alex Roan is, who they managed to piss off recently, all of it. We need to keep this under wraps until we can determine whether this was just a one-time occurrence. No reason for this to turn into a media frenzy."

Hyde brushed back his sandy colored hair and said, "What if we try and confront Roan directly on this? Sure, he's probably got some airtight alibi cooked up, given how long these bodies have been here. But it's worth a shot, right?"

"Too risky," Braddock decided after a moment of thought. "If he's behind this, we'll only tip him off. Roan's too smart to get his hands dirty, so he must have hired someone to do it. Confronting him about it openly would only make things harder."

"Not if I'm the only to do it," Chavez interjected. "Roan knows how the game works, you're right about that. But the one thing he can't resist is flaunting it about like some piece art. And he especially loves to do it front of *me*."

Hyde caught the note of disgust in her tone and knew there was something there that she would divulge to him later, when their partnership had made it past a year. He looked to Braddock, who pressed his lips together in a thin line on concentration, brow furrowed. The harsh angles of his face were more pronounced like this. He tried to ignore the nugget of envy he felt; for Chavez he gave it some serious thought while he was turned down almost immediately. That was the just reality of being a new guy in a profession were it meant your suggestions were sometimes brushed off while someone who's been there longer could make virtually the same suggestion and be granted the consideration.

After a moment, Braddock declared, "No. If you were to confront him about this, it'd only set off alarms. We can't afford to play fast and loose with this one, Chavez."

She nodded, but the disappointment was clear; Hyde figured she must have wanted to get Roan bad for whatever he'd done to her in the past. She looked ready to argue further when a blue van came to a screeching halt and a virtual one man news crew stepped out. She quietly groaned and Hyde was tempted to do the same.

"Good evening, ladies and gentlemen," the man spoke into a camera he held close to his rodent-like face, covered in facial hair. In what was clearly a practiced tone, he said: "It's that time once again. Where I take you beyond the 'official statements' and 'press conferences' in pursuit of the truth. Though I'm late, you can clearly see that some kind of horrific incident has taken place. And, surprise, surprise, the police are trying to keep it from you. Why? Because they don't want you to know what really goes on in our fair city of New Orleans. But never fear; Anthony Martin brings you the exclusive story, live, on this latest edition of 'What's Really Cooking.'"

Braddock sighed and pinched the bridge of his nose, clearly in no mood for any shenanigans (as he put it) tonight. "I'll go see what Dr. Marshall has to say about this, you two take care of this guy."

Easier said than done, both detectives thought at the same time; Anthony Martin was not someone who could easily be "taken care of." A former reporter for NBC, he was the station's fastest rising star with the highest ratings and following (there were people who *actually* found him *attractive*) until he broke a story that would have supposedly garnered national attention. According to the station's official statement, he falsified reports and sources and was promptly let go. His flock of followers soon abandoned him when his fame was taken away. He was said to be living in the very van where he kept his equipment.

His appearance supported the rumor; ripped and tattered shirt with faded jeans and worn out shoes. His brown hair, once slicked back, now spread haphazardly and oily, bangs hanging in front of his face. His small eyes were a dark contrast to his pale skin. Tony Martin was a shadow of his former self, now obsessed with "uncovering the truth" and "exposing the political cover-ups." Chavez would have honestly felt bad for him—part of her already did—if he didn't stir up trouble at crime scenes.

They approached cautiously, trying to appear as non-threatening as possible, when he tensed noticeably. He clutched his camera closer to his chest, his small eyes narrowing like an animal when it's being backed into a corner. His sharp gaze darted between them quickly, absentmindedly retreating back to his van.

"Tony," Chavez tried to sound as friendly as possible, "we just want to talk. And I bet you're willing to listen, right? A journalist never turns down a chance for an exclusive."

"And drink the Kool-Aid that has this entire city turn a blind eye to what's *really* going on?!" he snarled. "I don't think so, pigs! This is the second gang slaughtered this month, and I'm not about to let you cover that one up too!"

"Second?" repeated Hyde in a whisper, his gaze glancing to Chavez's for a moment. She met it with the same grim realization, but quickly hid it away behind a mask of professionalism. There had been another butchering like the one tonight, but someone had apparently covered it up. That wouldn't bode well for the top brass; it would only serve to validate Tony Martin and his crusade.

Martin noticed the slight hesitation and took advantage.

With speed uncommon to a man of his poor conditioning, he leapt into his van and slammed the door shut. Shuffling to the front seat, he started the engine and sped off into the distance. With a silent curse, they let him go in order to bring this new information to the captain. If there was another killing just like this one, then maybe there had been a survivor of that nightmare as well.

***

When Captain Thom Braddock was told of a case with too many similarities to one his own squad was working—coupled with the possibility those with the power to remove him from power had covered up the whole thing—he would normally look ready to blow a gasket. But he took the news in strides and decided it was best that they speak to Alex Roan; particularly after learning that both buildings had been purchased by him. The point of avoiding a direct confrontation (preventing another massacre from taking place) was now moot. Roan, or whoever he'd supposedly hired, had already struck twice. They were told the leading detective on the case was to meet them there.

When they pulled in front of the *Bête Noir*, there was already a squad car staking out the building. Leaning against the vehicle, his shaved head reflecting the brilliant flash of color from the neon sign, Marcus O'Mara smoked a cigarette down to the bud. He checked the watch on his right wrist and flicked the bud away. He simply stared at them for a moment, eyes the color of steel—neon light reflecting off of them, giving him an almost inhuman look—watching them, judging them.

O'Mara was well known amongst the precinct for his dislike of partners, preferring to go it alone. It made him very unpopular with his co-workers at the precinct, but no one could argue with his results; he had the highest arrest record of anyone on the squad. Renee Chavez had only ever seen him at his desk in the squad, going over old case files. This was going to be her first time watching him work.

"O'Mara," he thrust his hand outward, caramel skin shadowed by the darkness. Lean, but built, like a runner, and a shaven head carrying the shadow of black hair.

Renee took it first, "Chavez."

Jackson followed suit, "Hyde."

O'Mara eyes glinted with dim amusement, "Like the doctor or that pothead from *That 70s Show*?"

Hyde resisted the urge to roll his eyes, "Let's cut to the chase, shall we? We need to know everything about the first murder."

"Firstly, to call it murder is the most merciful thing you can do," O'Mara sighed. "But at least a slight pattern's been established. Last month, 911 received a call; the only thing they could make out were screams coming from one of the old department stores that had been destroyed by Katrina. When I went to investigate, it looked like someone decided to reopen the butcher's store down there. I heard you found a survivor this time?"

Renee injected herself into the conversation, "At the hospital, no ID, says *El Diablo* killed them." She carefully omitted the name of the hospital or the gender of their only witness. She knew O'Mara was probably holding something back, so she thought about doing the same. Hyde had agreed with her when they discussed their plan of action.

"That so," O'Mara rubbed his square jaw. "Maybe it was some kind of satanic ritual gone wrong."

"You're suggesting there's merit to their story?" Hyde's brow furrowed. "That the Devil or something was summoned and killed them because they didn't do everything right?"

"I'm just trying to get in the head of how this S.O.B. thinks."

"We've wasted enough time talking this over," Chavez declared. "Now I say we have a little chat with the man on all our minds, Alex Roan."

On that much, they chose to agree and headed for the inside of *Bête Noir*.

Chapter 5

Bête Noir was opened less than three months after Alex Roan first arrived in New Orleans. Originally a small office building in the downtown area, the club was only two floors high; an unassuming rectangular prism save for the neon sign. The ground floor where the regular customers—people looking for a few hours' escape from the hardships of everyday life—intermingled was bathed in neon lights of purple, red, green, etc. hanging from the ceiling. The bar sat on the far right side, its counter stretching across the entirety of the space, wine bottles of every vintage lined in rows beneath the menu. It took twelve men to tend to the customers; the smell of steak, burgers, hot dogs, etc. wafted through the air from the kitchen. A disc jockey was positioned antipode to the bar, playing the latest themes from the radio. In between the two, dozens of tables and booths were filled with couples enjoying romantic evenings, friends relishing in wiles of youth, and businessmen celebrating a deal going through. Next to the dining area, a dance floor glowed different shades of different colors, people wildly flailing around.

Even in this setting, a place where anyone could melt away into the ambiguity of a group this massive, the three detectives stood out. Chavez, Hyde, and O'Mara stood at the entrance of the club, adjusting to the atmosphere. The *bump, bump, bump* that could be heard outside became the loud, obnoxious, tones of dubstep. O'Mara noticeably grimaced, apparently not a fan, and followed the two detectives into a sea of people. On the far end of the club, an elevator stood guarded by a stiff in a suit.

The second floor of *Bête Noir* was reserved for "V.I.Ps" who were interested in more than what was presented here. It was generally believed that everything from drug use to sex happened up there. So, of course, Alex Roan made sure to invite the right kind of people (city officials, judges, and even the mayor, if you believed the rumors) to enjoy his "hospitality."

The stiff looked like a gorilla wrapped in a suit, his large arms and simian like posture only adding to the unusual air around him. He made the three of them for cops almost instantly and stood a little straighter, looking down at them. Chavez didn't miss the bulge on the side of his waste, no doubt a gun. He wouldn't be stupid enough to open fire on a crowded night like this, but she noticed Hyde right hand twitch in anticipation. He spoke in a gruff voice over the music, "Can I help you, officers?"

"We're here to see your boss," O'Mara met his gaze without fear.

"Mr. Roan's a busy man," the stiff said, eyes narrowing. "Make an appointment and he'll get back to you soon enough."

"Sorry, but I'm afraid 'Mr. Roan' will have to make an exception tonight. We're here on police business, and we have a few questions for him."

"Maybe you don't get how this works, son," the stiff tensed, arm reaching back towards the gun. "Maybe your little badges and pee shooters can get you into anyone else's joint without a warrant or probable cause, but not here. Unless I see some papers signed by a judge, you're not getting through here."

O'Mara steely eyes narrowed, and he looked ready to force his way through, when the elevators doors opened and out stepped the man of the hour himself: Alex Roan. In the light of the elevator—fluorescent instead of neon—Roan's tan skin was perfectly visible, eyes the color of jade tight with joy as he stepped out with two women, arms around their wastes, laughing. A silver suit that soon adjusted to the light of the room, neatly trimmed brown hair, a grin that revealed perfect teeth, and a face stuck between boyish charm and masculine maturity.

He stopped abruptly once his eye landed on Renee Chavez, his smile growing even wider (if that were possible) once his lady friends left to mingle. He stepped around the stiff, oblivious to the game of intimidation between him and O'Mara. He took her hand, "Renee, darling! It's been too long! What did do to earn the grace of your presence tonight?"

Chavez bit back the urge to punch him in that smug little face of his and simply put on an air of professionalism. "We have a few questions we'd like to ask you."

"I'm sorry, I can't hear you," he replied. "The music's too loud! Come on up to my office and we'll talk. You can even bring your friends!"

He turned back to the elevator and held it open for them, the stiff stepping aside to let them through. O'Mara gave him a mirthless smirk as he passed by, earning a scowl from the guard. Hyde stood on the opposite of Roan, wanting to be as far away from the man as possible. Roan insisted on Chavez being close to him, which she complied with, to her chagrin. The doors slid shut and isolated them from the music beating outside. The elevator rose to the second floor and they got off once the doors were opened.

They were in a hallway, a row of doors on either side; moans and the sound of skin slapping together could be heard from the rooms. The dark red carpet looked black in the dim lighting, Roan leading their party to a door at the end of the hallway. Rather than risk disturbing his guests and worrying them about the presence of the police, Roan remained quiet, but his demeanor still managed to speak volumes. Somewhere, in one of these rooms, there was someone with the political pull to make the lives of the three detectives a living nightmare. So as much as much as they wanted to see what dirt they could get on the occupants inside, they kept their gazes forward.

Roan opened the door to what seemed to pass for an office-in-progress and let them in first before shutting the door. The carpet was a brighter shade of red than in the hallway, walls covered in floral designs, pictures of Roan with several city officials, celebrities, and even patients at a children's hospital. Framed certificates, plaques, and awards for his many contributions to the community. A small bar sat to the left, surrounded by a couch, and two chairs. A large desk stood in the middle of the room, a lamp shining light over some documents (which he was quick to swipe into a drawer).

Leaning back in the chair, he grinned at them, "So how can I help the fine officers of the New Orleans Police Department?"

"We need your help, identifying a witness to a crime," Chavez said. O'Mara had opened his mouth to speak, but closed it with a frown, clearly not appreciating the interruption. She ignored him and pulled out her phone, bringing up the picture of the young the girl. She'd taken while she was being treated by the paramedics; it was close enough for an ID if he knew, but far enough so that Chavez wouldn't spook her. She watched Roan carefully as he scanned the photograph, gauging his reaction. Something flickered in his eyes a moment, the self-assured grin leaving his face.

He took a breath and whispered, "Monique."

"I'm sorry?"

"I know her," he said. "Monique Reynosa. She works as a waitress on weekends, paying her tuition."

"Good worker?" O'Mara asked.

"She doesn't like the work—who would—but she gives it everything, I wish I had more like her." Roan shook his head, putting the phone down and pushing it back to Chavez. To anyone else, it would have seemed like he was *actually* worried about Monique, but Chavez could see through his little act. She knew better than anyone how well Alex Roan could put on airs when benefitted him the most. He finally "gathered" himself and asked, "Is she all right?"

"As we said," O'Mara butted in before Chavez could answer. "She's a witness in a case. You said she was a waitress. Any customers ever get a little too 'friendly' with her?"

"Just the drunks," Roan snorted. "Much as I pride myself on my clientele, we do get an unsavory individual from time to time. They come in, drink as much as they can afford, and harass the staff. A few have been bounced and had their picture put up so we know not to let them back here. I can get you copies, if you like?"

"That won't be necessary," O'Mara jotted down the information.

"Actually," Hyde injected, "it will be."

There was a pregnant pause, O'Mara turning his steely, laser-like, gaze on Hyde, who met with no fear or intimidation. Chavez was pretty sure *this* was why O'Mara preferred working solo. Roan watched the exchange with amusement, though hid it well (from everyone but Chavez) behind a veil of concern for Monique.

"Mr. Roan," Chavez decided to take from there.

"Please, Renee," he smiled at her, their eyes meeting, her skin crawling like it the last time she met his gaze. "We know each other well enough by now, call me Alex."

"*Mr. Roan,*" she continued. "Monique, was she involved in any gang activity, or was she acquainted with anyone who was?"

"Not to my knowledge, all I knew about her was from what she did here, my employees only ever talk with each other. I am management after all. You'd have to ask one of the bartenders—Mackie! He'll know, he's got eyes and ears everywhere." Roan pressed a button and spoke, "Mackie, could you come up here for a moment?"

In no time flat, a tall African-American man entered the room; his black hair was little more than a shadow left by a haircut. His face was made of harsh angles, further exemplified by his deep frown, a scar running along his temple. A black shirt wrapped tightly around his torso, large arms poking through. Faded jeans and worn out shoes fit around his tree-like legs. He regarded the three detectives suspiciously before setting his eyes on his Roan.

"The police say Monique is a witness in an investigation," he explained. "I need you to tell them if she was involved in anything or behaving unusual lately."

Mackie sighed and scratched his head, "All I know is that she was hanging out with a few regulars. They looked like trouble, but they were always quiet, so I never bothered with them. But I always kept an eye on them. Is Monique all right?"

"She's fine," O'Mara replied. "These regulars, could you identify them?"

"Sure."

"Then we've got nothing more to talk about for now," O'Mara tucked his notepad into his pocket. "It's late and I'm sure you're both busy. We'll get out of your hair now."

"Please," Roan stood. "Don't hesitate to call if you have any questions, here's my card." He pulled out a small business card and handed it to O'Mara. He took it curtly and they turned to leave, being escorted by Mackie. Chavez's cell phone buzzed again; this time she checked it. It was one of her neighbors, Kira Massey, married and a mother of two (a boy and a girl), who looked after Chavez's home when did undercover work.

She answered, "Kira, everything all right?"

"I should be asking you that," she answered. Her voice possessed a Smokey quality that lent itself to a mystique that she didn't necessarily possess. "*You know who* is outside your house right now, waiting for you."

Renee felt as if someone had just thrown cold water in her face, a small shock working through her. She swallowed hard and tried to fight off the bubbling anger that dwelled in her stomach. *What the hell was* he *doing there?*

"Chavez," O'Mara snapped from the elevator. It took her a moment to realize she'd paused as soon as Kira passed on the information to her. She could feel her cheeks flare up from embarrassment. With all their gazes on her, she did the only thing she could.

Gathering herself, she spoke to Kayla: "Thanks for the heads-up, I'll take care of it later." Hanging up the phone, she continued toward the elevator, ignoring the curious stares she got from the three men. They went back to the ground floor and moved toward the exit. That's when she stopped again.

"Go on without me," she said over the loud music.

"What for?" O'Mara asked impatiently.

"Everything okay, Chavez?" Hyde asked.

"I'm fine, Jack, just need a little time to myself, besides, my shift's over," she showed him her watch. He checked his own and realized just how late it was. After assuring him that she'd get a cab home, he left, though he still seemed reluctant to leave her in Alex Roan's club. O'Mara left without a word, having apparently judged that she was too much trouble to deal with. In all honesty, she could hardly care what he thought of her. He had no idea what she would do to avoid having to with *him*.

After all, who in their right mind would want to go home after a frustrating day like this one and speak to their ex-husband?

Chapter 6

Renee's head was swimming in an ocean of deliria, eyes opening slowly; she blinked rapidly as they adjusted to the bright light in her face. She then realized that her hands were tied behind her back and her legs were tied to the chair. Despite the futility, she struggled against her confines, the ropes digging into her wrists. She thrashed around, succeeding only in knocking the chair over and kissing the ground with her face. She let out a groan but still struggled when the door opened.

In stepped none other than Alex Roan and the goon who'd knocked her out, both looking down at her from their positions. Anger bubbled in her stomach at her current predicament; they must have thought she looked pretty pathetic like this. Their eyes gleamed with icy amusement, Roan directing the goon to put her back in place. Her original balance restored, Roan took a seat across from her, smiling almost sadly at her. It made her want to kick him in the balls over and over.

Gone was Roan's college frat boy demeanor; in its place, a dangerous criminal who had just discovered a cop in his midst. His reaction told the story; this wasn't the first time a cop had managed to infiltrate his inner circle. But he'd make sure it was the last time she'd do it.

Renee did her best to block out the fear that threatened to swallow her, hiding behind the mask of anger. She might have been in a vulnerable position, but it would be a cold day in Hell before she allowed Alex Roan to garner a sense of superiority over her. Meeting his icy gazes with stubborn defiance, she readied herself for whatever he planned for her.

Chavez stared into the glass of red wine, oblivious to the world around her, her reflection in the red liquid mirror rippling gently with the vibrations of speakers. She hadn't taken a sip, only ordering it to keep from drawing attention. She had no interest in getting drunk and becoming easy prey for some would-be rapist. And she'd had enough one-night-stands in the months following her divorce. Thinking back, she hated the empty feeling she woke up to after every encounter. It only reminded her of how alone she truly was now.

She couldn't go home until she was sure *he* was no longer sitting on her front porch; if he was still as stubborn as ever, he'd be there all night. But she had to work in the morning—if she wasn't called in tonight—and couldn't look like she hadn't slept at all that night. Especially since O'Mara had caught her reminiscing in the hallway. Briefly, she wondered what Hyde had thought of her day-dreaming; did he think it made her unreliable?

Though she wouldn't have admitted it back upstairs, she was touched by his concern—he'd caught her uneasiness with the use of his first name. She hoped he wouldn't broach the subject in the morning.

"You gonna keep starting at that all day?" Mackie asked gruffly, his frown ever present. "If you're trying to fit in, it'd be helpful to put away a few drinks."

"I haven't had a drop of alcohol in months," she admitted. "And I'd rather not go to work in the morning with a hangover."

"Never stopped most of our regulars," he took out a rag and started cleaning a beer glass. This reminded her of one of those old black and white films she and her parents used to watch on certain dates. The thought filled her with a warmth and yearning she hadn't felt in what felt like a lifetime. With both of her parents gone, and no siblings, spouses, or children, she'd found herself feeling lonely in recent months. As things were now, her only friends were Kira Massey, and her husband, Donnie.

She had to admit she was a little jealous of Kira's stable marriage; she juggled that along with a job and two kids. But she trusted Kira with her secrets, her emotions; she trusted her to call the police if *he* didn't get the message and leave. She found her mind wandering back to her ex too often and decided to drown it out with a sip from her glass. She breathed deeply, foreign, yet familiar sensations coursing through her. The music began to die down and people started leaving.

"I was under the impression your club would be open until dawn," she took another sip.

"Not my club," he shrugged, "not my call. Mr. Roan sets the hours."

"Interesting," she drawled, her detective's intuition making note of the information. She checked the clock on wall; it was midnight. Considerably early for a nightclub to close down. If Roan wanted them out this "early", there must have been a good reason.

And the longer it kept away from her ex, the better.

***

Chavez remembered a case she worked back when she was uniform, a series of thefts at a local supermarket. Rather than money, an assortment of items (food nearing its expiration date, shaving gel and razors, wet naps and bottles of water, etc.) were stolen. The market manager was too cheap to buy security cameras that actually worked, so it all fell to cashier who locked up every night. The manager was convinced she was responsible, or at least in on it. Chavez and two other officers were there for five hours trying to figure out what exactly was going on. Every theory they came up with didn't add up; the thefts occurred every two to three days (the days the young girl closed the store).

When her colleagues gave up and were about to arrest the poor kid, Chavez heard someone shuffling in the back. When investigated the noise, she discovered a homeless man had taken refuge in the store. He admitted to being the one who stole the food and items; he lost his job thanks to the poor economy and was unable to pay for his house. He only stole food on the days the kid worked because she was new at the job, but was also careful to only take the items that were close to useless. In the end, the manager declined to press charges and offered the man a job to pay off the food he'd eaten and a place in the back while they both apologized to girl for the misunderstanding.

Thinking back on moments like those made Chavez smile; it reminded her that people weren't as vindictive as they seemed at first glance.

The only thing that left the manager, the cashier, and her colleagues confused was how no one had been aware of a homeless man living in a store. He explained that he avoided detection by staying in the bathroom; being the last person to enter the bathroom guaranteed no one would look for you. He'd explained it had been an accident; but that no one had come to get him when he fell asleep after walking all over town looking for a job. When no one called him out on it, he managed to eat the old meals just before they expired. She had to admit it was rather clever.

She'd been struck by the memory of that case when she decided she had to be here when Roan closed up *Bête Noir* for the night. It might have been the red wine talking (even if she'd only had one glass), but she knew Roan was lying about Monique Reynosa. He had her associates killed, just like the gang a month before, to send a message about anyone who wanted to muscle in on Roan's turf. A message all of New Orleans was supposed to take heed of: The higher you think you can climb, the harder the fall to reality would be.

She resolved to speak with Monique Reynosa as soon as she was able to handle visitors; meaning she didn't have much else to go on.

Which was how she ended up like this; being inside the ladies' room, waiting, and making sure the club was empty, before she ventured out. Luckily for her, it seemed Roan was too cheap to buy cameras for the bathrooms. That, or he didn't want to give the impression that he didn't trust his clientele when they were on the crapper. Either way, it worked out in her favor. She knew whatever she found wouldn't stick if she happened to discover anything illegal.

But if Roan knew he was no longer as secure as he thought he was, he might be prone to making mistakes.

In the darkness of the bathroom, she opened the stall and felt her way through the blackened room. Her eyes adjusted to the darkness by the time she reached the door, stepping further into the blackness. She made her way back into the main room, the dim lighting from the bar illuminating the shapes of the tables. The chairs had been folded and turned upside-down, the dance floor was nothing but a black rectangle, and the disc jockey's station was empty. In comparison to the earlier dancing, dining and DJ-ing, *Bête Noir* was dead.

Glancing across the room, she noticed the elevator, most likely turned off. She glanced around, searching for an entrance to a stairwell. Right behind the DJ's station was a door that could possibly what she was looking for. Just her luck, it was a custodian's closet. Scanning the dimly lit room, she found another door behind the bar and in the kitchen.

Testing the lock, she opened the door, a staircase leading to the second floor. She ascended the stairs and opened the door, finding herself in the hallway, the elevator visible along the wall from her angle. So far, so good, she thought with some confidence. She could still hear the moaning from the rooms—apparently "after hours" didn't apply to V.I.Ps. She decided to check out Roan's office.

Standing in front the door, she reached for the knob when sounds of an unknown origin were heard from behind it. Pausing briefly, she pressed her ear to the door and listened carefully. The sounds inside the room were unlike anything she'd ever heard before. She swallowed nervously as she listened in closely.

"What are you going to do about the girl?" asked a voice she didn't recognize, rough and gargling.

"Nothing," replied Alex Roan, "let the cops handle her. She doesn't know anything."

"It's dangerous to leave loose ends," the voice argued. "Eventually, they come undone and everything falls apart. And unlike you, I don't have the luxury of time."

"Relax," Roan replied, the oily smirk in his voice apparent. "All we need to is—" Roan stopped abruptly and then there was silence. Chavez felt her stomach tighten in anticipation of what was to come. Her heart began to beat faster and faster, waves of fear sending chills all over her body. She swallowed again and pushed off the door, preparing to leave.

Then it happened.

In an instant, the door exploded outward into a million little pieces, the impact sending Chavez flying through the air. She hit the elevator doors with a thud and crumpled in a heap on the floor. Her skull throbbed painfully as she tried to regain her footing, managed to sit up against the doors of the elevator. Shaking away the disorientation, she opened her eyes and focused on where Roan's office door had been. Her vision swayed back and forth before finally settling onto what was before her.

From the opening of the office, stood something that made her blink twice, then several times before realizing she wasn't crazy. Some kind of misshapen creature stood in gaping doorway, resembling a human-sized wasp. Two long, pincer-like arms stretched out to the floor, digging into the carpet, clawed hind legs supporting it. Its torso was large enough for two professional body builders; its ribcage was exposed, the bones protruding like spikes around the rapidly beating heart. Two large, black wings flailed rapidly every few minutes before settling on the back, its spinal column stick out along the way. Its head was round, two antennae standing tall, black compound eyes capturing her every movement carefully, mandibles flexing in every direction, saliva dripping from them to the floor.

Chavez felt her mouth drop, her eyes bug out (no pun intended) and her entire body stiffen in shock, disbelief, and (most prominently) fear. The creature studied her a moment before its facial features shifted, almost smiling, were it possible. A low growl emanated from its throat, an almost harsh laugh. She willed herself to reach for her gun, pulling from its holster and holding it close. Against her will, her traitorous body shuddered in fear, making her grip uneasy.

Chavez could feel her heart pounding in rapid succession. She felt like her lungs were paralyzed, and broke into a cold sweat. She gripped her gun with both hands tightly, careful not squeeze the trigger. She had to do something, fast, before that thing did God knows what to her.

"Don't be afraid," a voice echoed in her head, rebounding off her skull painfully. *"Just relax."*

"What the hell?" she breathed, head throbbing.

"This is the only way we can communicate while I'm in this form," the voice said in a soothing tone. *"There might be some discomfort, but I assure you, it won't last* long.*"*

She caught the sinister note of amusement in its tone and realized just who the voice belonged to.

Alex Roan.

She didn't know how, or why, but she knew that it was Roan, his voice was unmistakable. This wasp-like creature, red scale-like skin bright even in the shadowy hallway, was the very man she sought to bring down. The very man who found a way to manipulate the system in his favor. The very man who, years ago, tried to kill her when her cover had been blown. The very man who, as it turns out, wasn't even a *human.*

Her breath shuddered, "Roan? What the *hell* are *you*?!"

44

"I am," he chuckled mentally, reverberating in her mind, *"your Bête Noir."*

He was advancing on her, slowly, like a ravenous fox approached a cornered rabbit, compound eyes aimed directly at her own. The black pools of nothingness reflecting her own fearful expression. The closer Roan got to her, the more she backed into the elevator door, trying to push through into the metal box and get away from him as quickly as possible. She briefly remembered the stairwell to her right, wondering if she could make it. The added weight of fear made her body feel like it was of tens of thousands of pounds heavier

He was at the halfway point between his office and the elevator, his hungry gaze never leaving her. The saliva dripping from his mandibles pooled around the carpet, the greedy anticipation evident in his low posture. Around them, the moans and slapping of skin could still be heard, the occupants oblivious to world around outside the throes of passion. The thought that she might die while a bunch of old politicians were having sex around her pissed Chavez off. If she was going to die in the line of duty, the last thing she heard was definitely not going to be that.

Holding the gun with a more assured hand, she set her sights squarely on the rapidly beating heart; then she pulled the trigger. In a brief burst of flame, her bullet soared through the air, buzzing across the space to the heart. Instead of the anticipated splatter of blood, the bullet bounced off the heart and felt to the ground, crushed by the impact. She didn't have time to despair and instead fired off the rest of the clip. She aimed directly for Roan's exposed heart each time, failing miserably.

"Stop it!" he cackled, *"That tickles!"*

His laughter resonated throughout her mind, veins in her temples throbbing rapidly and painfully. She was sweating as she fought against the pain, Roan growing ever closer, his hungry gaze staring down at her. She had emptied her entire clip into his chest, each bullet bouncing off his heart. His wings buzzed excitedly, drooling profusely on her lower legs. Her skin crawled as he was so close to her face, some kind of tongue flicking outward. It swiped her cheek, savoring the taste of her skin.

She squeezed her eyes shut, not wanting to look into the eyes of an insect. Thoughts of her childhood, being stung by a wasp, how she'd carried an unconscious fear of bugs veiled in anger, passed her by. She thought of *him*, back to when he was the most important person in her life. Maybe she should have just gathered her courage and faced him instead of hiding out in Roan's club hoping to catch him in something illegal. Now she was about to die; just like those boys in theatre.

"El Diablo," Monique's voice whispered.

She wouldn't scream; she'd deny Roan the pleasure of hearing her scream, her admittance of fear. She waited for him to just get it over with when the elevator doors opened; she fell back just as she heard the report of a gun. The thunder-like sound echoed through the hall; Roan recoiled from the shot, his shoulder exploding. He released a high-pitched cry of pain before hunching low to pounce on the figure who'd seen fit to shoot him. He paused, regarding the newcomer in what seemed like annoyance.

In his dark pools, Chavez recognized the person who'd just saved her life, staring up at him in shock.

Reverend Michael Strauss stood in the elevator, a trench coat draped around his attire from earlier. His green eyes blazed with an icy fury that promised to freeze and burn Roan, jaw set firmly, reminding of her that comic book character, his name escaping her at the moment. She looked at the gun in his hand (were reverends even allowed to carry guns?). It appeared to be some variation of a Desert Eagle, runes designed along the barrel. Without taking his eyes off Roan, he knelt down to check on Chavez.

"It appears I made it just in time," he observed, somehow managing to project a fatherly air into his voice. "It was good idea to come check on Mr. Roan after all. Are you okay, detective?"

"I," she couldn't quite understand what was going on here. Just moments ago, she was about become a midnight meal for Alex Roan, whatever the hell he was. Now, she was alive, being comforted by Strauss. She didn't know how to react.

"Yes, I realize this might be a lot to take in, so please let me do the talking," he risked taking his eyes of Roan and smiled assuredly at her. He returned his stern gaze to the creature before him, "I believe you've had your fill of fun for tonight, Alexander."

The creature chuckled, shifting in what seemed like a painful process back into a human form. Roan stood before them stark naked, a pain grin plastered on his face. His breathing was labored, the wound in his shoulder already starting to heal. Once

46

he caught his breath, he chuckled, "Forgive me, Father. For I have sinned."

"There is no confessional on this Earth that could pardon whatever atrocities you've committed," Strauss snapped. "I've known you to be foolish in your time, but *you* of all 'people' should know better than to try and attack a police officer. That is a violation of the agreement."

"What am I to do when an armed prowler breaks into my office?" Roan asked, tone dripping with the defiance of a teenage boy.

If Strauss had not been a man of faith, Chavez was certain he might have shot him again.

"I will be taking Detective Chavez home," he holstered his weapon.

"Of course," Roan smiled. "Good night, Reverend, Renee." He turned to leave, the darkness his only censor from their eyes. "And by the way, it was John Constantine you were thinking of."

The doors to elevator closed shut.

***

Strauss took her hand, squeezing it gently, and led her out of *Bête Noir,* into the cool night air. He walked her over to his car, a black 2007 Volvo, unlocking the passenger's side and holding it open for her. Under normal circumstances, she would have brushed off the gesture, but tonight she was grateful. She slid into the seat, relaxing against the cool leather, and buckled herself in. Strauss slipped into the driver's side and started the car. Soon, they were cruising along the road to the freeway.

Even for The Big Easy, half-past midnight was a time where even an insomniac could find sleep. The streets were bare of any vehicles, sans a few, even fewer people out and about. For most of the ride, Chavez said nothing, her mind still making an attempt to piece everything she'd just seen together. Strauss was patient, giving her time.

It was only when he turned on her street that she spoke, "Wh-What was that?"

"That was," he sighed, eyes focused on the road ahead, "something that you weren't meant to see."

"Roan," she whispered. "He's . . . He's. . ."

"Not human, yes. I know this hard for you, but I'll be more than willing to answer your questions later. I have someone I need to speak to about this matter. In the morning, I'll come see you and provide as best an explanation as I can."

"But—" she tried to think of a proper argument. But all she wanted to do was close herself off for the night. The thought of being alone tonight frightened her, but it was better than allowing someone she hardly knew (even if he was reverend) see her any more vulnerable than they already had.

He pulled up to her house; *he* wasn't there and, for some reason, Chavez was disappointed. But there was no use dwelling on it right now, she needed to rest, all her energy from earlier that night leaving her. She dragged herself out of Strauss's car and walked to the door, the reverend walking her along the way. She unlocked the door and entered her house.

She turned to Strauss, "Thank you."

"Of course," he smiled at her. Nothing about his gazed passed judgment on her, deemed her unworthy of her badge. Only comforted her like a father would his daughter, like her own father had done many years earlier. He placed a comforting hand on her shoulder; she would later note two things. She felt warmer for some reason, and she was suddenly tired, but not willing to close her eyes just yet.

"I expect you to be at the station," she said as sternly as she could. "As early as 8:00 AM. I've got questions and you've got answers."

"I'll be there," he promised. "Good night and peaceful dreams, Detective."

"Night," she closed the door and turned on all the lights in her house, not trusting the shadows. Slipping off her shoes, she closed the door to her bedroom, a choked sob escaping her throat. So many emotions ran through her; embarrassment at being afraid and having to be saved; shock from what she had just seen, unwilling to trust that she wouldn't be visited by that nightmare in her dreams.

Most of all, she was crying out of the joy and relief that she was still alive, still here.

Chapter 7

The sun peeked through the windows of Chavez's house, rays of sunlight shining into her bedroom, urging her to wake up. She had barely been able to sleep that night, images of Roan, his insect-like face, staring at her, that tongue-like appendage licking her, *tasting* her. After a couple of hours, sleep took her. Fully awake, she began to wonder if it was all a dream.

Then she looked down as the sheen on her pants; a reminder of how close Alex Roan had been to killing her, of what he was. If not Reverend Strauss, she would have been consumed by her worst fear, figuratively and literally. She nearly tore the pants off of her and threw them in the garbage, returning to her bathroom to take a shower.

She punched the tile wall, a flash of pain shooting up her fist; humiliation and anger tied her stomach in a knot. She'd allowed Roan to see her vulnerable; she'd been afraid and had let it show for that sick bastard to see. Having seem him stark naked, she wondered briefly if he was aroused by her fear. The darkness covered everything below the wait, but that leering gaze was all the confirmation she needed. Even under warm water, her skin couldn't stop crawling.

The sight of bugs always made her skin crawl; just the way their bodies were built disturbed her; not to mention the things they were capable of. Spewing venom, their stingers, spreading disease, she both feared and hated insects. But that was neither here nor there at the moment.

All that mattered was that Strauss was going to give her answers today like he'd promised. She needed to tell Hyde what she'd seen last night, as well as Captain Braddock and Detective O'Mara. They weren't likely to believe her or even Strauss, but this wasn't something she could keep from them. It might cost Chavez her badge, but she couldn't take the risk they'd try the same thing she had. It was by sheer luck that the reverend had been there last night. There was no guarantee that he'd be there next time.

Stepping out of the shower, she quickly got dressed; a flannel shirt with the sleeves rolled up to her elbows, black jeans that hugged her thighs, and boots. She brushed her hair back, her badge fashioned into a necklace around her neck. Looking at herself in the mirror, she could still see the uncertainty in her gaze. She willed herself to morph her face into a mask, hiding her emotions from the world outside her home. Taking a deep breath, she grabbed her gun, holstering it at her side and stepped out of her house.

Kira Massey was watering her garden when she noticed her Chavez, "Renee! Good morning!"

"Morning, Kira," she replied with a false smile. "Thanks for the heads-up last night."

"What are friends for?" she brushed her hair back; curly and ginger, falling just pass her shoulder blades. Her jade eyes glowed brightly in the morning light, dimples showing in her smile, which revealed perfect teeth. She kept a well-maintained physique for a woman who'd been through two pregnancies (if what you heard on television was to be believed). She went jogging around the neighborhood every Monday through Friday morning. Her long legs were further pronounced in the denim shorts she wore this morning. A button-up shirt was draped around her nicely. Chavez checked her peripheral vision for any of the local neighborhood kids; she'd caught them drooling over her once or twice a week. Hormones were a dangerous thing at that age.

Renee had first met Kira when she and her then-husband moved next door, Kira being pregnant with her second child (her son). Ricardo and Donnie had hit it off, inviting them to dinner at their place. A friendship between the four of them blossomed, maintained even after the birth of her son while already raising a daughter. She was someone Chavez knew she could count on. And her presence was very welcomed after the horrible nightmare she suffered through last night.

"How are the kids?" Chavez asked.

"Still kids," Kira sighed.

"You'll be wishing were the case when they're teenagers, trust me."

50

"I'll just remind them that there's a cop living right next door."

Chavez managed to force a laugh out at the joke, when Hyde pulled up to her house, parking in the driveway. He got out and greeted Kira before turning to Chavez, his expression stern, "I've been trying to reach you all morning, you all right?"

"Yeah, I'm fine," she lied. "What's up?"

Hyde glanced at Kira, who caught the unspoken request: *Give us a moment, please.* She turned off the hose and rolled up to her house before looking back, a mischievous smile on her face, "He's a cute one, Renee! You better pounce on him before someone else does."

Her attempt at mortifying them an apparent success, she went inside.

"If she only knew," Hyde said breathlessly, managing a grim smile. "We just got called in for another murder. Captain wants us there ASAP."

"How many?"

"Just one," he answered, sounding about as relieved as anyone could be in this situation. "They wouldn't say who, which probably means the body's too torn up to ID off the bat."

Chavez was suddenly back in the hallway on the upper floor of *Bête Noir*, staring into the black pools of Alex Roan, her own terrified expression looking back at her. She watched his pincer-like arms, wondering just how much damage they were capable of. She could hear his voice in her mind, the pain that accompanied the intrusion.

"I am you're Bête Noir."

"Renee!" Hyde broke through her haze, looking at her worriedly. "Is everything all right? You were spacing out." She must have been if he had to call her by her first name. Instead of answering, she got into the car and he started the engine.
***

The French Quarter, also known as the *Vieux Carrè*, was the oldest neighborhood in New Orleans. A landmark in Louisiana's history, many of the notable buildings were a reflection of Spanish colonial architecture built in the late 18th century. Chavez lived just outside the Quarter, so she often walked the streets on her days off. They seemed different now that she was on duty, her eyes searching for anything that stood out. She watched the neighborhood go by when Hyde turned on to the neighborhood's heart, Bourbon Street.

From her seat in the car, she could see the crowd that had gathered, news trucks parked and reporters in front of cameramen. She wordlessly cursed, eyes scanning the area for any sign of Tony Martin. Hyde parked the car and they got out, working their way through the crowd. Like sharks to the smell of blood, the reporters picked them out from the rest and swarmed. Ignoring their questions, they located the crime scene, Forensics already prepped and ready to process.

Ducking under the police tape, they stepped into one of the local bars, closed down during the day. Captain Braddock glanced at them while he questioned the owner, the man looking somewhat bored. Maybe this wasn't the first time someone had been killed in his shop. That didn't bode well for their investigation; the last two murder scenes had been old, abandoned buildings that had been damaged by Katrina. Given what Hyde told her, this wasn't connected to either case.

The scene had been set up behind the counter, leading into the kitchen, a trail of blood starting at the door. Chavez and Hyde went around back and entered the kitchen, Dr. Grace Marshall meeting them. She appeared to have just finished her cursory examination of the body, her expression grim. Their view of the body was blocked by a stove, the legs visible. Pulling on latex gloves, they prepared to examine the body.

Circling around the stove, Chavez felt the entire world melt away.

For the second time in twelve hours, her blood chilled to point that her body froze entirely. She sucked in a breath, her mind unable to possibly comprehend what was in front of her. She managed to swallow nervously, her stomach feeling queasy. Staring intently at the body, she ignored everyone else.

She stared at the mangled body of Reverend Michael Strauss.

Chapter 8

Blood painted an abstract image on the wall where the body was rested against. His shirt was ripped open, a deep gash running from his left shoulder to his right hip, internal organs poking through. His arms lay useless at his sides, spread out as if in a placating gesture. His head was tilted in the same questioning angle as the teen on stage at the theatre. His green eyes which had been so full of kind life stared back with a dull expression, mouth slightly ajar. He looked as though he'd been at peace when he was killed; suggesting perhaps he knew it was coming. Whatever the reason, Chavez had an entirely new problem.

With Michael Strauss dead, there was no one left to explain to her the things she'd seen last night. Crouching down beside his body, she couldn't help but ask, "What were you going to tell me? Who did you meet and how did it end up like this?"

Forensics snapped photos of the body at different angles, as well as the blood trail, and made way for the coroner's crew to take the body. They handled it with the same care they would handle a child; he was a man of God after all. That notion alone probably made this whole thing uncomfortable for everyone here.

Especially when you considered that this was one of the last places anyone would expect to find a reverend. Bourbon Street was more commonly known for its wild bars and strip clubs than anything that would attract a Baptist reverend. More often than not, people tended to remember how you died—more importantly, *where* you died—instead of how you lived. Nowadays, people were already starting to lose faith in the church, so this wouldn't do them any favors. That was, assuming, any of those vultures outside knew the identity of the victim.

Strauss has saved Chavez's life; the least she could do for him was make sure his good name stayed just that.

"I need to speak with Braddock," she decided out loud.

"What for?" Hyde asked, crouched on the other side of Strauss's body had been, searching for clues. She hesitated for the briefest of moments, weighing her options. She had—to her knowledge—been the last person to speak with the reverend before his death. The minute she relayed this to Braddock, he was likely to take her off the case. Unless she told him *everything*.

She'd already decided she would bring them in on this, but without a clear idea of what she was dealing with, and no one to back up her claims, she wasn't so sure now.

"Because—" she began when Braddock entered the room, his features set into a stern frown. She'd seen that look only a few times in her years working under him, and it was never a good sign. And it usually meant he was in no mood to suffer foolish nonsense. That was exactly what he would call what she about to tell him.

"What's up, Captain?" Hyde asked.

"Monique Reynosa," he answered, "She's finally calmed down. I need one of you to speak with her."

"I'll go," Chavez replied. "I think she'll respond better to me, no offense Hyde." Hyde shrugged and resumed his examination of the crime scene. Chavez followed the captain outside to the streets, where the media was waiting. Braddock took a deep breath and prepared himself; he'd dealt with reporters long enough to know the routine. He sped up and met them head on while Chavez got into the car and headed for the Ochsner Medical Center.

***

Renee hated hospitals; her father had died while in surgery after a couple of joy riders slammed into him on the freeway. She remembered sitting in the waiting room with her mother, clutching her hand tightly, and waiting for the inevitable. The doctor hadn't minced words. Her father had bled out from massive internal bleeding caused by the crash. By some cruel twist of fate, the passengers in the other car were relatively unharmed; one was cut up pretty bad and had a broken leg; another would never regain complete use of their arm.

Of course, their parents were well connected and made the charges disappear; they'd offered to pay the hospital bills and funeral. Given that she was still a cadet at the time and her mother had been a housewife, Renee swallowed her pride (along a mouthful of curses) and accepted the money. After the funeral, she returned to the academy and focused on her studies with even greater fervor. She isolated herself from the rest of her class, preferring not to take to risks with late nights drinking and getting into fights. When she graduated, she was top of her class.

She'd done it all to make her father proud, to honor his memory by making sure kids with privileged upbringings couldn't just have Mommy and Daddy buy their way out of trouble. Her mother had passed away two years ago, leaving her by herself— back then she at least had Ricardo to ease her pain. With a deep sigh, she let go of all those memories and focused on what was happening now.

Getting off the elevator, she walked into the sterilized environment of the hospital wing. The nurse's station was on the far end of the room; a short and stocky woman dressed in red scrubs looked up. Her face was red and round, reminding her of a balloon, hair braided. Narrow eyes watched her, nose scrunching up as she approached. "Can I help you?"

"I'm Detective Chavez," she held up her badge for her to see. "I'm here to see Monique Reynosa. Brought in last night, in a hysterical state I was told she was coherent."

She squinted her eyes at the badge, scrutinizing it, to make certain it was genuine. She decided that it was and directed to Monique's room, an orderly finishing up his business there and leaving. In comparison to how she first looked when Renee had seen her, she was much less wild now. Her hair was tied in a bun, eyes no longer wide with horror, completely calm and stiff compared to her earlier state. Her eyes lit up in recognition when she took notice of Renee, the nurse leaving them to speak privately.

"Remember me? I'm Detective Renee Chavez," Renee took a seat, smiling.

Monique smiled and nodded, sitting up a little straighter. Given everything she'd been through since last night, it must have been nice to see a familiar face. It was a common ground both woman found themselves on. After her own experience last night, Renee was in need of her own sense of familiarity. Speaking to a witness, getting the facts, finding the bad guy; that was familiar to her, her comfort zone.

"Last night," she began, taking out a note pad, pen ready, "what exactly happened?"

Now her demeanor changed completely; her eyes hardened; grasping the sheets tightly; her posture grew rigid. This was a girl who'd been told everything she witnessed last night was nothing more than a hallucination. They probably ran a blood test to make sure there were no drugs in her system. She made a mental note to ask for the results later. Right now she needed to show this girl that she was on her side.

"Monique, I don't know what the doctors must have told you, but I want you to tell me what you saw," she grasped her hand. "I'm not here to judge you."

"You won't believe me," she muttered bitterly. "I don't even believe me."

Chavez smiled, "I know you're skeptical. But try me. You might be surprised."

Chapter 9

Monique Reynosa had led a relatively normal life leading up to today, though the journey to that life had apparently been a rough one. It had all started with a car ride, a family of four happily spending time together while the world outside passed by. Games, jokes, songs, it was all any child could really ask for at the time, in that mindset of youth and innocence (ignorance, some might call it). Beside Monique, her older brother, José grinned at her with a mouth full of gummy worms, eliciting an excited shriek from her. She remembered the joy that shined in her parents' eyes, still in love after ten years of marriage.

When her father turned on the corner to the next street, time had slowed down for them, at least that was how Monique remembered it.

Looking out the window, she saw three young men, dressed in baggy jeans, wearing bandanas around their foreheads, jackets and skull caps. She remembered their faces, their calm, robotic, regard fixed on their car. Something about them frightened little Monique, but it was that same unknown that kept pressuring her to watch them, to remember each of their faces, down to the smallest detail. She noticed two men in particular who stood out amongst the rest. One of them met her eyes, smiling at her in earnest, reassuring her.

That would be the last time—in what seemed like forever when she thought back to it—that Monique Reynosa would ever smile.

What happened next flew by in a haze of images, sounds, and disconnect. Screams echoed loudly before fading into silence, her vision inverted for the briefest moment, she felt a pair of arms wrap around, removing her from the car. José screamed frantically, voice stretched out into a high pitched squeal. Then there were lights on the ceiling, passing by while unseen shapes conversed with each other, escorting her somewhere. Finally, everything seemed to connect again when she woke up in a bed, nurses attending to her.

When the nurse noticed her eyes were open, she called for the doctor, who, despite his physical condition, seemed out of breath. He shined a light in her eyes, asking her to follow it; she did her best, enough to convince them both she was awake.

"Hello, Monique," the doctor greeted her. "How are you feeling?"

They had gone to great lengths to make sure she was comfortable, until she asked for her parents and brother. The doctor exchanged a glance with the nurse before clearing his throat, "I'm sorry to have to tell you this, but you were in an accident; you and your brother made it out okay, but your parents..."

After the doctor had explained everything to her (in as best a way as anyone could tell a little girl her parents were dead) they told her that her brother had been taken into foster care. She would also be placed in a home when she was discharged, the staff doing their best to ease the transition for her. All the while, she said nothing, her mind replaying the news over and over again. When she was declared fit enough to leave the hospital, she was placed into foster care.

Over the course of the next few years, she would be moved from home to home, the reason varying each time. All of her pent up anger and despair being unleashed in the most unhealthy ways. When she was eleven, she broke the nose of a girl who tried to bully her. Two years later, she stole her foster parents' car and slammed it into a tree. When she was fifteen, she broke a glass vase over her foster father's skull (the bastard deserved it for beating her with a broom, though, if the report was to be believed). A year later, she met a family that was willing to put her up, in spite of her faults.

No matter how many times she screwed up, they never gave up on her; she started thinking they were some kind of emotional masochists. Eventually, her anger began to subside and she started opening up to them. They helped her get her grades in order, and she passed with flying colors into college. She majored in medicine of all things, she wanted to be a nurse. But when her parents began struggling financially, she turned to Alex Roan.

Roan had been looking for a waitress for his new club, *Bête Noir*, and she fit the bill; despite knowing his reputation, she worked for him. It wasn't glamorous and the customers were jerks, but the money was good and she was never asked to do anything degrading or illicit. She'd worked there for six months when she got a customer she never expected.

His skin color reminded her of sand, black hair cut low, a small patch of hair beneath his chin, eyes the color of coffee. He wore a red neon shirt with black denims, large arms resting on the counter. His face was tightened into a scowl, eyes scanning the club for something. He sat on the far end of the dining area, emitting an unapproachable aura. When she walked up to take his order, she knew it was *him*; even though they hadn't seen each other in such a long time, she knew in her heart.

She waited until her left, telling Mackie she was going on a break, and followed him outside. He stopped at a street corner to have a smoke when she approached him. When he saw her, his eyes narrowed, "You want something?"

"José," she breathed, hoping, praying that it wasn't a mistake. He seemed taken aback by her knowledge of his name, eyes now focused on her, trying to remember where he'd seen here before. She squirmed under his gaze but held her ground, her beating frantically.

"M-Monique?" his eyes widened and mouth dropped open, the cigarette falling out to the ground. She nodded vigorously, her vision becoming blurry. Without warning, she threw herself into his arms, quietly sobbing.

She'd found him; she'd found her brother.

After her shift was over, they'd spent the rest of the night catching up over cups of hot chocolate. José's life had not been an easy one; her troubles were nothing compared to his trials. He'd fallen in one with a would-be gang, but promised they weren't trouble.

When she'd first been introduced to them, she wasn't convinced.

Despite their rough appearance, José's friends were well-mannered and tipped generously; still, people watched them carefully. José waved them off as bigots, but Monique couldn't quite agree, she'd been nervous about his friends as well. They came off as the type of guys who liked looking for trouble. The same kind of guys who'd killed their parents. Pushing the thought aside, she continued to socialize with them, though she could tell that Mackie didn't approve.

He was too nice to say anything, but the frown on his face when they started acting up said enough. He watched them like a hawk, ever ready to claw out their eyes if they should ever look at anything valuable for too long. José seemed aware of Mackie's distrust, but never said anything about it.

Things remained quiet for the most part, until one day, when José brought in a friend who seemed more interested in the club's earnings than actually dining.

"Figure a place like this," he began, eyes roaming over the bar, dining area, and dance platform, "pulls in a weekly average in the quintuples, maybe twice that on weekends. So who's to say Mr. Roan would miss a few hundred dollars missing from the revenue every now and then?"

"No," she'd told José when it was just the two of them.

"*Mi Hermana,*" he touched her shoulder, "It's only a few hundreds, not like he'd miss it."

"You want me to *steal* from Mr. Roan," she hissed. "The only reason I'm paying my tuition is because of this job. If I get caught, Mackie will—"

"But you won't," he insisted. "And he won't hurt you. I promise."

The look in his eyes had stayed with her, the sureness that what they were doing held no consequences for either of them. She also remembered the guilt; the heartache she'd felt when she'd first realized it was him. His struggles through life since the day was engraved into his expression, posture, demeanor, etc. Monique had lived comparatively well when she thought about what José must have gone through. She weighed her options and decided to do it.

A decision she would soon come to regret.

The first week, she had only taken one hundred dollars a night, coming up with five hundred by the end of the week. It had been enough for whatever they were doing, and Mackie hadn't caught on apparently. But things soon took a turn for the worst when, a month earlier, they started asking for more money.

José had tried to reason with them that she was already risking enough by taking five hundred dollars every week. But they said they needed more—started demanding, even threatening. She wasn't sure if her brother knew, but someone had started following her around campus for the entirety of that month, sitting on her classes, watching her in the dorms. When she confronted him about it and threatened to go to the police, the stalker grabbed rough and shoved her against the wall.

"Either you get the money," he whispered, his breath reeking of cigarettes, "or I come back here and collect something else."

Though she agreed, José had been furious when he'd found out, but they'd assured him that it wouldn't happen again. They were right, she'd been scared enough to go through with it.

This time, she took a large enough amount that wouldn't go unnoticed and met them and predetermined rendezvous. The old theatre, its foundation weakened after Katrina, was hollowed out and barren, the perfect place to make an exchange. And it had been going along smoothly until a bone-chilling scream echoed throughout the darkness. She only remembered bits and pieces of what happened next. An animal like roar, blood flying everywhere, someone being strung up.

When it was all over, she stayed frozen in her hiding spot, too afraid of what might happen if she chose to reveal herself while that thing was still out there.

***

Renee listened intently as Monique recounted her tale, shuddering at the memory of what occurred. Her brother had dragged her into some kind of gang and forced her to steal from Alex Roan of all people. In return for her trouble, she witnessed José and his friends being torn apart by something that defied a world dominated by scientific fact and logic. Renee felt the familiar sensation of fear crawl up and down her spine like cockroach, its prickly limbs digging into her. "I believe you, Monique. I know you think I'm just trying to humor you, but I believe you. I'm going to need your help to find whoever, or whatever, did this."

Monique laid her head on the pillow left by the orderly, unable to fathom that someone actually believed her. That maybe she wasn't as crazy as she (and probably others) thought, that her brother might not have died for nothing. She locked eyes with Renee and opened her mouth her to speak, her face freezing and eyes widening. A choking sound escaped her throat and her hands flew straight to her neck, trying to fight the invisible hold. When she started to convulse, Renee saw that her tongue was swollen.

"Nurse!" she cried, "Nurse! Someone! Get in here, now!"

The nurse from the station raced inside, "What's going on?"

"She choking, I think she's having some kind of allergic reaction," she explained hastily. She noticed the pillow and grabbed from beneath Monique's head; it smelled of peanuts. She thought back to orderly, and cursed herself for not making note of his appearance sooner. The nurse had called in the doctor, kicking her out. She glanced around the ward to find a figure turning his head away from the scene and walking out.

"Freeze!" she shouted after him, sprinting into the hallway.

She rounded one corner just in time to see him disappear behind another. She followed after him, skillfully dodging on-lookers (this wasn't the first time a suspect ran), turning on the corner to just barely miss him again. She turned another corner, nearly crashing into a cart carrying trays of food for the patients. She watched as a door to the stairwell closed and ran inside, just in time to see the orderly circling downward like something in a sink. She followed him, skipping a few steps in order to catch up.

Reaching the ground floor, she saw him running toward the entrance. Speeding across the lobby, she exited the hospital, and nearly jumped down the stairs. He was within reach now, a little more and she had him. Reaching her hand out, she grabbed him by the shoulder, barely getting a look at his face. He managed to shake her off just as car slammed into her, sending her to the ground, out cold.

She grunted as the goon's fist collided with her stomach, brass knuckles digging deeper than his flesh ones could. She could taste the metallic flavor of blood rising in the back of her throat, but she swallowed it. When he stopped, she glared at him with a swollen right eye, chest heaving, arms bound overhead. The goon briefly ceased his assault and examined his handy work. He stepped aside to allow her a better view of Alex Roan.

"Renee," he drawled out her name, his tone that of scolding parent. "It's late. I'm tired, you're tired, and my pal here

is exhausted. *A simple answer to a simple question. That's all it'll take for this to end."*

" 'S-Screw you," she wheezed..

"Tsk, tsk," he waved a finger in front of her. "Language, young lady. Keep that up and I'll have to spank you." She glowered at him, blood boiling; she responded to his goading with a mixture of mucus and blood from her lips to his cheek. Wiping his face, he used that same hand to smack her with a resounding thwack!

"Now, now," he cooed, "a woman shouldn't display such vulgar behavior. Now, one more time: Who is your informant? I know you've got one."

Renee kept her lips in a thin line.

Roan nodded to his man and stepped outside of the room while the goon resumed his beating. She grunted with each strike that connected and did her best to ignore the pain. When she wouldn't break under the force of the blows, he picked up a lead pipe and prepared to swing.

The door was kicked off its hinges as two officers stormed inside and wrestled the goon to the ground. They stepped into the room and quickly checked his corners, one of them holstering his weapon and undoing the bindings. Her body fell limp against him, her vision fading into the darkness.

Renee opened her eyes, staring up at a ceiling, and realized she was lying in a hospital bed, a nurse checking on her. She tried to sit up, the nurse and her body protesting in response. A sharp pain on her side stopped her mid-way and she laid back down. Her head throbbed painfully, wrapped in a bandage. It took her a moment to remember just what happened.

"Monique!" she sat up straight, more paining biting at her side.

"Detective," the nurse scolded, "please, calm down."

"Monique Reynosa," she ignored her. "Where is she?"

"Please, you have to—"

She didn't have time for this, "Where. Is. She?"

The nurse hesitated, eyes shining with remorse, "I'm afraid Ms. Reynosa didn't make it."

Chapter 10

The three detectives all sat in a silent circle around Braddock's desk, the latter letting their reports sink in. Monique Reynosa, the only survivor and witness to last night's brutal slayings, was dead, killed by what appeared to have been a hit man. A hit man who knew about her peanut allergy; a pro.

Chavez was released from the hospital after the doctor determined nothing had been broken. She had some bruising on her left side where the car had struck her, but the damage was minor and had since subsided. Hyde picked her up and they returned to the precinct, informing both Braddock and O'Mara of the developments she made. Their reaction to learning the only witness in their case was dead was the same. Chavez watched the veins in O'Mara's head throb angrily.

"You screwed up," his laser-like gaze was aimed for her. "You should have made the guy as soon as you saw him. Instead, you let him kill our only witness."

Maybe it was because she was in enough pain, or because she could find no reason to disagree with him, but Chavez simply glared at him. She thought O'Mara seemed a little too angry; although losing a witness in a case was never easy, his reaction was a little too hostile. She could understand to an extent, losing a witness in a case after a month of no breaks was tough. He needed someone to blame, but she wouldn't back down from the clear challenge blazing in his eyes.

"If anyone's to blame," Braddock stepped in. "It's me. I should have put officers outside her room just in case something like this happened. Sounds like this guy's a professional; Roan's the only one I know who could have hired him. And given what you've just shared with us, Chavez, we've got motive. If it was Roan, then maybe the guy at hospital was also responsible for the butchering last night."

"But what about last month?" Hyde asked. "What do we know about the victims?" At this, they all turned to O'Mara, still glaring at Chavez, who gladly returned the favor.

"No ID on two of them," he answered. "But the third man was Nathan Vega, 27, a repeat offender. Nothing about him stood out, but there was talk that he was planning to climb the ranks. And do it fast. Guess Roan decided to eliminate him before he became an actual threat."

"And this time?" Braddock leaned back in his chair.

"Bruce Raymond, 29," Hyde answered.

O'Mara took his eyes off Chavez, brow furrowing, "My informants tell me he's got history with Vega. That they 'come from the same place.' Could mean this is about more than just Alex Roan. If they're from the same place, my bet is a few old enemies followed them."

"Alright," Braddock demanded their attention "O'Mara, I want you to look into these slayings, but keep Chavez and Hyde in the loop. Gather whatever information you can on Vega and Raymond. Where they're from, who wanted them dead, and who had the means to do it. Until you bring something concrete, work under the assumption that Roan's our primary suspect."

O'Mara nodded and left, sparing a sharp look at Chavez. She huffed and crossed her arms while Braddock dished out their assignments. Something told her she already knew was it was.

"I want the two of you to work Strauss's murder. Find out if he had any connection to Monique Reynosa. I don't buy him dying and her biting just hours apart from each other."

"Captain," Renee knew he wouldn't like this, but telling him meant it wouldn't bite her in the ass later. "You should know that I was the last person to see Reverend Strauss alive."

The captain sat there a moment, soaking in the knowledge like a sponge. The lines running along his face grew harsher as he frowned. His age was becoming more noticeable lately; it made both detectives feel uneasy. He pinched the bridge of his nose, eyes tightly shut; he wasn't sure how much longer he could do this.

"Never took you for the type to seek religious guidance, Detective," Braddock folded his hands over his desk.

"We didn't meet at a church, sir," she looked him in the eye now. Her chest tightened; she felt like a little girl telling her father she'd done something wrong. "Last night, we... ran into each other at Roan's club."

"I'm guessing neither Hyde nor O'Mara knew about this."

"No. After we were done questioning Roan, I decided to stay behind, so I could uncover something. Around closing time, I ran into the reverend and he gave me a lift home."

His gaze narrowed, conveying the air of a man not to be taken lightly, regardless of his age. Displeasure written clearly on his face, he said nothing. She took the silence as a cue for her to continue, "I was supposed to meet him this morning, and he was coming here to speak with you."

"And someone didn't want the meeting to take place?"

"It looks that way."

She wasn't making things easier for him—any of them, in fact—and it made her feel guilty. Glancing at Hyde, who looked more pensive than usual, she felt like a jackass. They hadn't been together long, but a partnership was strong so long as there was a proper amount of trust. Renee didn't want him thinking she didn't trust him, but couldn't think of anything to say.

Braddock leveled his sternest gaze on her, "Just work the case, alright? Go to the church and ask around. But don't make me regret not taking you off this case, Chavez. I expect a full report on my desk by tonight. Dismissed."

Chavez and Hyde nodded, stood, and left the office.

***

"Hyde," she began, struggling to get the words out. Renee Chavez was not the type of person who apologized often. She was much too stubborn for that; just ask Mary Beckett, who'd been her Maid of Honor at her and Ricardo's wedding. She'd punched her in the face once, breaking her nose. Of course, she had a good reason. Seems like there was always one where she was concerned. But this was different; being partners meant you were placing your life into someone else's hands. It wasn't something meant to be taken lightly in their line of work, and she needed Hyde to know that was how she felt, her pride be damned.

"You don't have to apologize," he answered, eyes on the road. The drive to the church had been a quiet one up to now. "I know you well enough by now to sense that more went on last night than what you told the captain. You don't want to talk about it and that's fine with me. I'm not going to force it out of you, but I just wish you'd have a little more faith in me."

There was something in his tone, and it made her feel like the absolute worst at the moment. *I have faith in you, Jackson,* her mind commanded her mouth to say, but the last time she'd said that, she'd been terribly disappointed. She felt it was better if Hyde knew it without her having to tell him. Still, she owed him something to prove it.

"I'm sorry."

Hyde smiled at her, genuine warmth in his eyes, "Don't worry about it."

As they pulled into the church parking lot, they could see several shapes and figures dressed in black attire. News travelled fast in the Big Easy, it seemed. Dozens of church goers were out in force, mourning the loss of their reverend. It made their job all the more difficult as a result.

Getting out of the car, they went around back and knocked on the door; the same woman who had been there yesterday greeted them. This time, she let them in without hesitation. Her round face was wet with tears, eyes red, but she managed to compose herself and led them to the office where Michael Strauss had worked for the benefit of their congregation. Before she let them pass, she looked them both in the eye.

"Is... is it true?" she sucked in a shaky breath. "Reverend Strauss, was he found in a bar?"

Under normal circumstances, Detective Chavez wouldn't have divulged sensitive material, but this woman was need of some comfort. "Yes, we have found his... body in the kitchen of a bar on Bourbon Street. But I'm sure you more than anyone would know that he was probably their trying to help some poor soul."

The woman's expression changed somewhat, almost smiling at her, composing herself enough to let them pass. The secretary had apparently heard them outside, meeting them when they stepped into the hallway. Her own eyes were red with tears streaks down her cheeks. Sniffling, she lead them to what had once been Strauss's office, his things already packed up.

"Thank you," she said once the door was closed. "Every one of us is just devastated; first Simon, now Reverend Strauss. The media will no doubt try to make where he was found and why more important than everything he's done for our community. But I'd rather not bore you. You're here to ask questions, aren't you?"

"We realize this isn't the most convenient of times," Hyde sat down in front of her desk. "Did the reverend have any next of kin that need notification?"

"None that I'm aware of," she answered. "He mentioned that his parents both passed some years ago."

"What about his personal life?"

"He wasn't seeing anyone, I don't even think he was dating," she didn't look too disappointed by that. "He had a friend who's been staying here for the last six months, I never learned his name. He's out now, but I'm sure he'll want to contact you as soon as possible if he knows anything."

"This friend got anything that might help us identify him if he chooses to come to the station?" Hyde jotted down each bit of information on the notepad.

"Trust me, you'll know him when you see him."

"Care to elaborate?" Chavez asked.

"He was—" The phone started ringing, the caller ID belonging to a local school. "I'm sorry," she answered it. "Hello . . . Yes, this is Joy's mother... I see, did you call her father?" The pursing of her lips suggested she didn't like the answer, "No it's no trouble, I'll be right there. I'm sorry, detectives, but I go pick up my daughter. She locked herself in a closet because of some bullies. And, of course, her father is too busy to go check on her, even though he's closer."

"It doesn't get any easier does it?" Chavez smiled, feeling a small sense of kinship with the woman when it came to spouses (or ex-spouses in her case). "About Strauss's friend?"

"He wore a mask," she answered, distracted by the situation with her daughter. "I'm sorry, I really have to go."

They followed her out of the church, deciding to leave the mourners in peace (and because they doubted anyone knew Strauss as well as his secretary and "masked friend"). Getting back in the car, they sat there for a moment, weighing their options.

"So where to now?" Hyde asked.

"I know a guy," she said. "Maurice LeBlanc. He runs a pond shop on St. Thomas Development. He tends to be in the know whenever something significant happens. Look Hyde, it'll be better if I go alone."

"Why's that?"

"It's complicated."

He nodded, "'All right, but the second something goes wrong—"

"You'll be the first one I call," she offered him a warm smile.

***

Maurice LeBlanc was an odd kind of pond shop owner. He arrived in New Orleans nearly two years ago, establishing himself amongst a specific clientele. Unlike a typical pond shop owner, LeBlanc had no use for money (outside conventional needs) and often traded items for information. The kind of information that you didn't want certain people knowing. Depending on the information, he sold it to the "right" people for a reasonable price.

His preference of knowledge over cash was displayed by the name of his shop; *Celui Qui Réfléchit* (He Who Ponders).

A building that sat at the end of St. Thomas Development's south, on the edge of the Mississippi River, the shop was small cube-like building. Painted the stone grey, the neon sign flashed with the colors of Mardi Gras: purple, green, gold, and white. Leblanc was the kind of man who liked to advertise his location.

Renee had used his seemingly unquenchable thirst for knowledge in the past; it had helped her collar some truly dangerous men. LeBlanc had a code; if you were part of organized crime and the worst you did was rough someone up for protection money, he'd trade with you. But if you were a serial killer, rapist, child molester, or all of the above, he'd put you on the police's radar. Still, he did it for a price.

Hyde dropped her off at her house, where she took her own car down to his shop, waiting for a chance to speak with him privately. He preferred not to have his reputation be too closely associated with the police. "Bad for business," he told her once. She had to agree; the less of a connection to the police he had, the more trustworthy he would seem to criminals (the irony of the statement wasn't lost on her).

The sun rested at the edge of the coast, the darkness of the night settling in; the neon sign shined brighter, along with the rest of the city. When his last customer left, Renee got out of the car and walked up to the shop. She behind her and in front of her, she walked inside. The interior of *Celui Qui Réfléchit* always struck her as abnormal.

The shelves were lined with stereos, CD, DVD, and Blu-Ray players, game consoles, and even a VCR that seemed like the last of its kind. Beneath the shelves were televisions of various sizes and designs, barbeque pits and grills, lawn ornaments, and some bed frames. All this and more were lined neatly along black tile floor that reflected the florescent lights on the ceiling. The walls were the color of sand, their texture just as rough, and a counter sat next to the door. Behind the glass were an assortment of items listed as "NOT FOR SALE" in bold red letters.

When she opened the door, a small bell rang, alerting the shopkeeper to her presence. Maurice LeBlanc was a middle-aged black man with a beer belly, a balding scalp, large arms jiggling with fat, round cheeks, and intuitive eyes. He wore a blue flannel button shirt, black pants, and an old watch on his right wrist.

He looked up from his register and smiled when he saw her, "Renee Chavez! Why I haven't seen you here since we caught the Tulane University Rapist." He spoke with a slightly regional dialect native to New Orleans. However, his tone suggested he was not the healthiest of people.

"You mean *me and my partner*, right?" she smiled, much in way someone smiled at the antics of friend. She liked to think he was someone she could call a friend most days.

"I'm not your partner?" he scratched his head.

"Much as I love our rapport, I'm here on official business."

"'Course you are," he laughed. "You wouldn't be here otherwise. I imagine it has something to do with the reverend who was killed this morning. I heard about on the news. Real shame, Michael was a nice guy."

"You knew him?" she raised a brow.

"My mother's part of his little flock. Couldn't get enough of the guy. I never saw the appeal, then again, I'm not what you'd call the 'religious' sort, so . . ."

"Heard anything interesting, lately?"

"Nothing worth reporting. Business has been real slow today. Don't know too many people who'd associate themselves with a guy who kills reverends."

The bell rang again, and Renee glanced out of the corner of her vision; three men stood in the doorway. They were varying shades of color, with different hairstyles—one was clean shaven, short black hair. The other's head was shaven and all clean of facial hair. The one in the middle looked like a wild man, thick beard and long hair. She searched LeBlanc's face for an indication on how to handle these guys.

He swallowed nervously; they weren't the type liked cops.

She silently walked away from the counter to rummage through shop's inventory. The wild man approached the counter, eyeing LeBlanc suspiciously. The other two watched her, following her movements.

"LeBlanc," the wild man nodded. "You got what we asked for?"

"I do, but it's now's not the ideal time to—"

The wild man reached inside his pocket and slapped a roll of bills on to the counter. LeBlanc managed to avoid looking at Renee, but she could feel his unease. She had a feeling those three could as well. He took the bills and put them into his pocket, crouched down behind the counter, and came back up with a box. The other two briefly abandoned their vigil of her and helped inspect the products.

Renee took the opportunity to leave the store, committing their appearances to memory. She knew LeBlanc also ran an illegal dealership from his shop; if she saw it, she'd have to arrest him, regardless of how valuable his information was.

Behind her, the door opened, footsteps behind her; just what she needed. This was supposed to be a simple meeting with LeBlanc, how did turn into this. Picking up her pace, she almost at her car when he gripped her shoulder, roughly turning her around. When he was in full view, she rammed her elbow into his face. He recoiled, grunting, and tried to attack her; she used his momentum to slam his head into the backdoor of her car. A barely noticeable dent appeared when she pulled him back and tossed him to the ground.

The second one tried to jump her from the side, but she grabbed his incoming fist and threw him over her shoulder, using his weight against him. He landed on the ground with a thud, taking hold of her arm and refusing to let go. This distraction allowed the final member of the trio to rush her, slamming his fist into her bruised side. Pain resonated in that spot for a moment before spreading to her entire body. It paralyzed her long enough for two of them to grab her arms and force her on her knees.

"She's a cop!"

"Like that matters, we'll gut her all the same."

"Why kill her right away? Been a while since I've had a little fun with a lady this fine."

"Come on, guys!" LeBlanc came lumbering out of his shop. Clearly he wished someone else was in his place, but he was a man of principal. "You don't wanna do that. You'll spend the rest of your lives looking over your shoulders. You know how cops are."

"Then maybe we should make sure there are no witnesses!" the wild man yelled, releasing Renee while his subordinate grabbed her arms. Using the bat he'd gotten from inside the store, he cracked it over LeBlanc's skull. He swayed for a little while before collapsing into a heap on the ground. The glee that was present on his face seemed to unlock something in him. Suddenly, he and his two goons changed, just like Roan had changed.

This time, instead of a wasp-like creature, she found herself in the presence of three Quadra-pedal creatures, Leo-like blue faces, elongated teeth, glowing yellow eyes. Their "manes" looked like scales shimmering in the moonlight, their bodies a darkish blue fur, claws on the end of their arms and feet. Tails swished about furiously, tuffs of fur on the ends. The leader howled joyously into the night sky. Then, it turned its gaze on her, something dark and foreboding shining its bright eyes.

She struggled with even greater urgency; a useless gesture she knew, but wouldn't go through this, not again. The leader stood on his hind legs, grinning with a malicious hunger at her, and showing off his sharp row of fangs.

"No use, sweetheart," he taunted, voice deepened by the transformation, "It's party time."

"Looks like she's seen us before," one of them said.

"Think she might be a Hunter?"

"It doesn't matter," the leader said. "We have our fun, then we kill her." He stalked up to her, his two lackeys presenting her to him, bringing his clawed finger under her chin. He forced her to look up at him, relishing in the horror he was about to unleash.

She defied him with a determined expression, still struggling against her captors; she wasn't going to be that helpless damsel she was last night. Out of nowhere, something collided with the Leo-like monster's face, blood spurting out of his right eye. Taking a step back, he howled in rage and pain, bringing a hand to the offending object current blocking his vision. Getting a better look at, it look like a . . . throwing star?

His two partners released her and she backed against her car, weapon pulled from its holster. When the two took up defensive positions around their boss, she followed their angry, frightened, gazes. Beneath the nearest street lamp stood someone readily waiting to meet these monsters head on.

Getting a closer look, his appearance struck her immediately; just a boy. A boy in a skull mask.

Chapter 11

Renee would later note that it had, perhaps, not been an apt description of him at the time. He was a boy, a teenager to precise, with a mask covering the lower half of his face starting at the bridge of the nose, a skull printed on the black fabric. But that was not the only thing she made note of at the time. He wore what appeared to be a black combat suit, uniquely designed. Between the segments, red fabric was visible; on his gloves, a raised white skeletal hand pattern. *Tabi* boots, shin and forearm guards, a kanji printed on his right shoulder pad, and an assortment of weapons along his waist. On his back, he sported a katana. The combat suit covered his entire body sans the upper half of his face and short black, feathery, hair, waving off to the right. Blue eyes, slanted and wolf-like, glared furiously at the three creatures, emitting an aura that froze them in their tracks.

Between his fingers, two throwing stars were twisted around in a kind of therapeutic fashion.

The trio of beasts who'd been ready to tear her apart had all but forgotten her in favor of this new target. But she realized something immediately, reading their body language. Despite their fierce façades, she could see the nervousness in their postures. The tenseness in their stances and their eyes darting around, searching for an escape. They were afraid of this young man.

Without a word, he reached behind his back to grasp the hilt of his katana, drawing the blade from its sheath. Under the light of the streetlamp, the katana gleamed, blinding them for a brief moment. That was all the opening the boy needed before he launched himself forward, moving faster than Renee's eyes could follow.

The next thing she knew, blood was spewing from the torso of one of the creatures, its cry of pain echoing into the night. The sound of steel cutting flesh and cracking bones made her queasy, but she couldn't look away. She was too dumbfounded by what she was watching.

The boy ripped his katana from the creature and let it fall to the ground, blood pooling around it, shifting back into a human form. Renee and the two creatures stood completely still for a moment, watching the body, then looking back to the masked boy. He turned his glare on the remaining two, striking a stance, katana gleaming crimson from the blood.

The second goon roared, "You! Bastard!!!"

He lunged forward, claws outstretched, jaw open and fangs visible, eyes wide with crazed fury. If she had blinked, Renee would have missed his quick dispatching of the monster, cutting it clean in half. The expression of fury twisted into one of shock, frozen on his face. Blood splattered on the ground in abstract fashion. When the boy looked up, he briefly locked eyes with Renee.

Heart drumming against her chest, she waited for him to make the next move. The masked boy returned his attention to the only remaining punk left. He reverted to his human form, throwing star still stuck in his face, backing away from the masked boy.

"You son of a bitch!" he roared. "You're gonna pay for this! You hear me?!" He turned and ran as fast he could down the street, the boy making an attempt to follow him. Not wanting to risk this fight involving innocent bystanders, she took control of her body and aimed her gun. She fired a warning shot off into the night, stopping the boy in his tracks. He rested the katana on his shoulder and looked at her with an inquisitive look, contrasting the fury she'd seen earlier.

"I'm pretty sure you missed him," his tone was casual, befitting a boy his age.

"I wasn't aiming for him," she answered automatically.

"Then why were you firing?" he frowned in confusion. "A gun isn't a toy."

It took her a moment to find her words; she was utterly confused now. "I was aiming for *you.*"

"What!" he shrieked. "W-Why?!"

"You just killed two people!" she snapped, gesturing to the two dead bodies. She didn't know why she was arguing with him, but not a lot of things were making at the moment. In the past 48 hours, she'd seen criminals transform into creatures out of fairy tales, nearly been killed, and had been saved by the most unlikely of individuals.

"B-But they were going to hurt you!" he reasoned, stepping toward her.

"Drop your weapon!" she ordered, aiming squarely for him.

His eyes widened and he threw his arms up to shield himself, "Don't shoot me! I'm not going to hurt you!"

"Then," she growled, "Drop. Your. Weapon."

It took a moment for him to realize she was referring to his katana and it finally dawned on him. He raised his free hand in complacence and slowly sheathed the blade, detaching it from his suit and placing it on the ground. Renee brought her gun close to her chest as she stood on her feet. He approached her, trying to appear as friendly as possible, when she snapped her handcuffs on his wrists.

"You're under arrest."

"F-For w-what?" he looked at his cuffed wrists disbelievingly.

"Murder," she narrowed her eyes. "You have the right to remain silent."

"B-But I was trying to help you!"

"Save it for the judge. Anything you say can and *will* be used against you in a court of law. You have the right to an attorney; if you cannot afford one, one will be presented to you."

She walked him over to the car, opening the back door and pushing his head down as he slid inside. He didn't seem to understand what was going on and glanced around nervously; hard to believe he'd just sliced apart two monsters. A groaning from behind reminded of her LeBlanc.

"Maurice!" she slammed the door on the boy and ran to his side, helping him to a sitting position. His eyes slowly skimmed over his surroundings, shaking away the disorientation.

"Renee," he slurred. "You okay?"

"I'm fine," she smiled. "Thanks for what you did. I know you're not the type to get involved."

"I got a code," he smiled awkwardly. "Never turn my back on woman in trouble. I'm not like those little punks."

She blinked, "You're one of them?"

"Not exactly," he rubbed the back of his head nervously. "Real sorry I never told ya. Not the kind of thing that's easy to explain."

"I would have thought you were crazy anyway."

"Yeah... well, I'm really sorry I couldn't do more for ya."

"You did more than most people would," she patted his shoulder. "Thank you."

He observed the scene before him, "Looks like I missed quite a show."

"I got the guy responsible. I'm gonna take him to the station."

"You sure you wanna do that?" he scratched his head. "He saved you. That should count for something, right? Defense of a third person?"

"I'm not really arresting him for murder," she told him. "I just need a reason to hold him until I can get this sorted out. There's already a serial killer on the loose and a dead reverend, last thing people need is some kid in a skull mask carrying a bunch of swords and throwing stars around."

"Guess you got a point," LeBlanc rubbed the sore spot on his head. "Just take it easy on him, he's a real nice guy. Anyway, to make up for the mess, I'll let you have the next three visits for free. You can ask me anything you want. And trust me, after talking with the kid, you *will* have questions."

"I'll take you up on that," she chuckled.

"And just because I'm really sorry, I'll let you know just who that kid you got in the back of car is. Name's Zero Ozawa. I'm sure you're wondering just who he really is, but that's a really long story itself."

"Night, Maurice," she picked put the katana and walked back to her car. She replaced the mask of professionalism, watching the young boy in the backseat. This Zero Ozawa was a character, all right. She threw the katana in the trunk and got behind the wheel.

"Is Maurice okay?" asked Zero.

"He's fine," she replied curtly.

"That's good," the boy nodded. "He's a really good guy. Hey, shouldn't we go after the one that got away."

"I'll get him eventually," she started the engine, glancing at the kid in her mirror. He seemed relatively uncertain about what was happening, staring out into the night as they drove to the station. She shook her head in disbelief, thinking with a small amount of amusement: *Way to ruin that badass image you had going for you, kid.*

***

Being this close to Halloween usually meant that NOPD precinct would be swarming with the most unusual cases. Cultists, sexual predators, people who claimed they saw ghosts in their backyard, the works. There was even a pool to see who could bring in the strangest case (whatever passed for strange in the Big Easy). Suffice to say, they were used to things that were out of the ordinary. Still, when Chavez brought Zero Ozawa into the precinct, it felt like time had stopped for the second time that night.

Every officer stared at her as she dragged the kid through the squad room, towards interrogation. She ignored their stares and stopped by her and Hyde's station, her partner staring at her incredulously. She handed him the katana, along with the other weapons confiscated when she brought him in, and proceeded to take Ozawa to interrogation.

"Chavez?"

"Hyde, sorry for not calling you," she kept her tone business-like. "But I'm pretty sure I just won the pool. I'm going to be chatting with Mr. Zero Ozawa"—she pulled him forward, and he bowed in response—"for a while. Have the labs run a scan on his weapon, once they get the blood cleaned off."

"Okay, what are you people looking at—" Braddock started as he emerged from his office, taking in Ozawa's appearance. The masked boy smiled in return, inclining in another bow. He dragged his palm over his face, "It's going to be one of *those* nights, eh Chavez?"

"You have no idea, Captain," she yanked Ozawa along to the interrogation room. She ignored the buzzing of the squad, huffing in annoyance. She opened the door to reveal a small green room, dimly lit, a barred window offering a view of the city through the tinted glass. A lone table sat in the middle of the room, two chairs on opposite sides. She sat on him down on the side facing the two-way mirror, where anyone could observe them (she imagined the whole squad was watching by now).

He drummed his fingers along the table, glancing around the room, his gaze settling on hers, blue eyes glinting with a question. She observed him with equal curiosity; she couldn't a handle on this kid. Having been a detective for as long as she had, she'd seen some unusual things (though what she'd witnessed in the past twenty-four hours left an impression all its own), but this guy was something else entirely.

"You know my name," he spoke first. "But I don't know yours."

"Detective Chavez."

"Detective?" he tilted his head to the left. "That's a pretty odd name."

If he was trying to piss her off, he was on the right track.

"I could say the same for you. What kind of a name is Zero?"

"It's mine."

"Your parents must not have had high hopes for you, then."

For a moment—Renee didn't know how—she felt the atmosphere around him change, growing harsher. Ozawa's expression tightened, meaning she'd hit a sore spot. Now she had a place where she could apply the pressure.

"I wonder what they'd think if they saw you gutting people like you did tonight."

"They'd probably think the same thing your parents must have thought when you told them you wanted to be an officer."

A familiar anger started boiling in her blood and she narrowed her eyes into cat-like slits. Ozawa's eyes widened for a second before narrowing also, his expression more inquisitive, as though he'd seen something. Then tension in the room was thick enough to shatter the two-way mirror she was sure the entire squad was observing behind. They stared at each other for what seemed like hours when only seconds passed by. Then Ozawa nodded and stood up.

"Sit down," she ordered. "You're not going anywhere."

"Detective, I have no intention of harming you," he said. "But I do believe something must be done about what you're going through." The small *clank* of handcuffs hitting the table made her look down, then up it again. Ozawa checked his wrists before grabbing the chair and jamming it beneath the doorknob. Three seconds later, someone (probably Hyde or Braddock) started pounding on the door. In just as much time, the masked teen closed the distance between them and cupped her face in his hands.

They were relatively the same height, so she could look him square in his blue eyes, eyes that were somehow shimmering. She felt trapped, could feel a small blush at the proximity, and cursed herself for it. This was a police precinct, the one place where they were supposed to have an advantage over them. Now, she was at the mercy of some kid in a costume, her mind lost in a sea of dizziness.

Just as she was lowered into the chair, the door was forced open, Marcus O'Mara (of all people) taking Ozawa down with ease while everything around her faded into black.

Chapter 12

The doctors examined the extent of Renee's injuries and decided it was better if she stayed overnight; she had three cracked ribs, a minor concussion, and a black eye. She had, of course, protested, but her superior threatened to make it an order before he left. Now she was in the hospital (by some cruel twist of fate, she was certain it was the same hospital her father had died in), arms crossed over her chest, mind wandering. She couldn't ignore the bitter taste of humiliation in the back of her throat, its taste harsher than blood. Renee stared out the window to find the city of New Orleans alive with celebration.

It seemed like there was always something to celebrate in the Big Easy, but she was certainly in no mood for it tonight. Months of hard work—infiltrating Roan's organization, climbing through the ranks at a snail's pace, getting the names of his contacts—all of it had been for nothing. Thinking back on it, she realized the "contacts" she'd been given were nothing more than competition. The last of which had been busted tonight, meaning she was no longer of any use to him. Roan has used the police, had used her *to tighten his hold on the city.*

Now, she was lying in hospital bed, her husband, probably worried sick about her, and felt like shit. Gritting her teeth, it was she could do to fight the anger that threatened to burst through. She'd get that bastard for this, make Alex Roan pay way or the other. Right now, she needed to get out of here, go home and make sure her husband was safe. If Roan knew about her, the chances were high that he knew she was married.

She wouldn't let Roan's thugs lay a hand on Ricardo; she promised herself to never let anything like this happen to her again.

Some promises, Chavez realized, were harder to keep than most, even if they were to yourself. Not that she was one to make excuses, but she'd been very emotional that night; back then, she'd have never thought things like what she'd seen in the past day were possible. Alex Roan and three unnamed punks being able to change into monsters (as well as Maurice LeBlanc, though she'd hardly call him a monster). Nearly being killed by said monsters, only to be saved by the last people she thought would come to her aid (considering she barely knew one and had no idea about the other). And, as of what she guessed was an hour ago, being knocked out by looking into the eyes of some kid.

Chavez was lying in a bed in one of the bunks reserved for officers who were working late shifts and too tired to go home (unofficially, they also stayed here because of personal issues). She adjusted into a sitting position and shook away the remaining dizziness, getting out of bed. She opened the door just in time to see Hyde walking her way.

"Renee!" he actually smiled; he must have been really worried. She would reflect on how touched she was later, after she finished what she started.

"Where's the kid?"

"Still in interrogation, we've got two guards watching him. Keeps asking how you're doing. Almost sounds concerned."

She nodded, "I'll show him."

Ignoring Hyde's protests, she stormed through the precinct, scaring the rookie officers out of her way. Once she reached interrogation, she opened the door, ready for round two. Zero Ozawa noticed her arrival and seemed almost relieved. Sitting across from him was none other than Marcus O'Mara, an eyebrow raised in her direction. It was the closest to surprised she'd seen from him in the short time they'd worked together.

"Detective!" the boy beamed. "I'm glad to see you woke up so quickly. You *are* the one Michael was talking about!"

Michael? she thought. *He couldn't mean . . .*

"You're tougher than I gave you credit for, Chavez," O'Mara looked down at the file in his hands. "I suppose you want to take it from here? Be my guest." He got up, file in hand, and left the room, leaving the stench of unease with the two of them.

Chavez sat down, unsure how to approach this, whatever it was. For all she knew, this boy could have been the one who killed Strauss. Her mind flashed back to that katana, how easily it had cut through those two monsters when her bullets had been useless against Roan.

84

Something like that would have no trouble cutting through the human anatomy.

But then she was struck by a memory from earlier that day, at the church with Strauss's secretary. She said that the reverend had no friends save for one that wore a mask. And that she'd "know him when she saw him."

"You knew Michael Strauss?"

His eyes dimmed slightly, "Yes, we met in Germany when he was tending to his parents' graves and I was... following a lead on something. He helped me set up shop here in New Orleans. Before you ask, I had nothing to do with his death, but I am responsible. We were supposed to meet in the bar where he was found, but I was too late. If I had been there for him, he might not be..."

"Why were you meeting him?"

"To talk about you, it seemed" his gaze grew sharper, again wolf-like, like he was looking through her. This time, the feeling was different, it was like she could feel tendrils reaching into her space, studying something about her. Her head was starting to spin, but she held on, glaring at the boy. He smirked behind his mask, "We spoke on the phone after he dropped you off. Told me that you were made aware."

"Aware of what?"

"Aware that the world turns in a different direction than you thought it did. After he was killed, I went to LeBlanc's to get some information, when I happened upon you. You're welcome for saving you by the way."

"Go to Hell."

"Never been there *myself*, but I think one my ancestors did," his expression changed again, becoming playful and nostalgic. It just made her want to rip that mask off him and stuff it in his throat to make him shut up. "But that's of little consequence. Right now, I need to tell you something. It's very important that I get my weapons back. If I don't, things are going to get messy."

"Like they aren't already?" she asked. "You slice three people up like it was a natural thing to do, and you're dressed like something out of cheap graphic novel. Besides, why should I believe a word of what you're telling me?"

"Aside from the fact that you've *already* seen *them*? You have no reason to trust me, but I am not your enemy. I only want to help you and keep people safe. I can also tell you that it was, very likely, that a *Mononoke* killed those people."

"A what?"

"*Kuso!* Forget what I just told you, it's not important." For a moment, he looked panicked, and it intrigued her. *Mononoke?* What the hell was that supposed to mean?

Before she could press him more—not that she was buying all this—someone knocked on the two-way mirror, beckoning her forth. She paused for a moment, looking squarely into Ozawa's eyes, searching for any reason to doubt his story. His gaze never wavered, never yielded any of the secrets it was hiding. She stood and left the room, walking into observation.

Captain Braddock stood in the room with Hyde and Marcus O'Mara, the latter's focus never leaving Ozawa. She could tell by looking at them that they didn't believe a single thing he said. She had been racking her mind for a way to tell about what she'd seen and now that they had heard it, they thought it was crazy.

"Is it true what he said?" Braddock asked. "You were attacked?"

Chavez nodded.

"What do we do now? We don't have anything to hold him on unless the labs tell me that sword of his was used to kill Michael Strauss or commit those murders."

"How about assault of a police officer?" suggested O'Mara. "Whatever he did to Chavez knocked her out cold. You really want to let this guy walk out of here with all that stuff we found."

Braddock glared at the floor, weighing his options.

"If I could make a suggestion."

Zero Ozawa stood in front of the mirror starting at what, from his side, should have been his own reflection. But he knew better, that he was addressing the four officers in the room. Blue eyes roamed over each of them. He briefly inspected each of them for a moment before settling his gaze on the captain. Braddock flipped a switch, cutting off power to the interrogation room. This allowed Ozawa to look at them properly, arms behind his back.

He looked ready to say something when two officers walked into observation, looking confused. They'd been sent to collect the bodies left outside LeBlanc's pond shop; from the looks on their faces, something went wrong. Just what they needed at the moment.

"Detective Chavez," one of them scratched his head. "About those bodies you wanted us to pick up for the coroner's office. You sure they were outside the pond shop?"

"Yes," Chavez frowned. "Something wrong?"

"When we got there, there was nothing there, no signs of any struggle or that the bodies had been dragged off somewhere. Curiously, the only unusual thing we did find were piles of ash. Odd, considering there were no chimneys in the area."

***

Dr. Grace Marshall was not in the best of moods right now.

It was one thing, being woken up and dragged to a crime scene and finding nothing. Now she was in interrogation, sitting across from, quite frankly, the most eccentrically dressed person she'd ever met. In addition to Forensic Pathology, Marshall had earned a degree in Criminal Psychology. Thom Braddock figured that made her the most qualified person to extract any useful information from Zero Ozawa. At the very least, it would be an enlightening discussion to be sure.

"All right, Mr. Ozawa," he cracked his neck. "Where are the bodies?"

"Right where I left them."

"Lying isn't going to help you."

"I'm not lying," he replied. "There right there, you just have to take a *closer* look."

From observation, Captain Braddock and Detectives Chavez, Hyde, and O'Mara watched intently, each exchanging glances at one another. This kid was on some kind of high, they all thought simultaneously. At least, that was what the cop in Chavez was saying, but she wasn't so sure anymore.

"Mr. Ozawa," Dr. Marshall addressed him, looking up from her notes. "Tell me, why do you wear that mask? In my experience, skulls are commonly associated with death. Are you a killer?"

"No," he grinned, acting like a little kid who knew something no one else did. "I wear it because I think it looks cool."

"Acting smart isn't going to help things, Zero," Marshall sounded like a mother scolding her son. "You may have helped Detective Chavez, but that doesn't make what you did right?"

Zero glared at her, "Don't patronize me. I'm not a child. I'm sixteen, I'll have you know. And of course I know the difference between what's right and what's wrong. I'm pretty sure it's *your* system that's gotten confused over the years. Anyway, when I can have *Araguru-getsu-ga* back?"

"Your sword?" she asked. "I can guess from the name, that it's a family heirloom. You realize you won't get back your weapons until we clear this matter up.

"That's the same thing they said to me back in Bangkok. Let me tell you, it wasn't easy getting them back. The cops there aren't as... 'lenient.'"

She changed the subject, "You said a '*Mononoke*' was responsible for the killings? Care to enlighten us as to what you know."

"Classic misdirection. You think if I tell you, it'll create a bond or something between us, right? That you'll understand me a little bit better and we'll be friends? Trust me, doctor, I like you, but you're wasting your time trying to get inside my head. Believe me when I say it's not worth it. Being up there would drive you insane!"

"Like it's driven you?"

Zero didn't respond, just smiled at her from behind his mask, and refusing to answer any more questions.

Braddock knocked on the glass; Marshall gathered her papers and bid Zero farewell. He led her, Hyde, and Chavez to his office. O'Mara left to work his own case a little while longer before his shift was over. Chavez muttered a "thanks" for what he'd done for her before, to which he simply nodded. It made all the more curious about, considering he looked ready to rip her a new one for what happened with Monique.

But none of that mattered right now; she had too many questions running through her mind at the moment. Why had Michael Strauss been killed, and did it have anything to do with Monique Reynosa's death like the captain suspected? What was a *Mononoke?* Was that the name of the creatures Alex Roan and those three punks could turn into? Who was Zero Ozawa anyway, and what did he have to do with any of this? For now, she decided it was best to let it all be filed away in her mind. She'd sort it out later.

Once they were inside the captain's office, he shut the door behind them and took a seat. Hands forming a pyramid over his desk, he made his decision: "Will let him stew in holding for the night before going at him in the morning. I'll call the D.A. in the morning and see what he wants to do about it. 'Til then, go home, all of you, we've got enough to worry about already. There are still killers on the loose out there."

"Sir," Chavez spoke up. "I'll stay, someone's got to watch Ozawa and I don't have anyone waiting up for me."

"Neither do I, but I'm too old for these overnighters so I'll take you up on that. The rest you, get out of here."

Chapter 13

Zero Ozawa sat, crossed-legged, in the holding cell, ignoring the stares from passers-by (he was more than used to it by now). His forearms were stretched out in front of him, middle and ring fingers curled inward, index, pinky, and thumb outstretched. His eyes were closed, his breathing slow and steady, and his senses tuned to everything around him. He could hear each footstep and determine the weight of whomever passed him by; which in turn helped him decide on said person's gender. He could smell the air through his mask, the stale donuts passed their expiration dates, fresh coffee (honey-nut) being poured into a cup.

He could also feel *its* presence in the building; a *Mononoke*.

Yes, it seemed there was someone who didn't want Zero to make it out of this precinct, and whomever they were, they were well-informed. Either they were paying off someone with an intimate knowledge of the police, or this person was high up in the chain of command. In Zero's experience, it was usually the latter, but he remained optimistic. He needed to warn the police that a demon was in the building? But he couldn't; the two worlds weren't ready to collide just yet.

Thus was the burden he carried of being a Hunter, especially one born to the Ozawa clan, perhaps the most notorious Hunters in all of Asia, if not the world. Since the Edo period, his clan had slain a fair amount of *Mononoke*, their legend spreading across the country and quickly growing with each kill. It didn't take long for them to become the most hated and feared of any Hunter in any region of time period. Of course, there was the occasional gross exaggeration, but they were only stories. Neither were ever encouraged or discouraged as fact or fiction; the less their enemies knew, the greater the advantage.

Though the fact that someone had sent an assassin after him this soon was flattering; he hadn't even been locked up twenty-four hours!

That alone provided him with more than enough information; someone didn't want to leave his fate to the courts. Whomever it was had to have known about Zero the moment he was brought in by Detective Chavez. Which could have been any number of people in the squad room or in the halls when they first arrived. They were likely responsible for why Zero had his own cell rather than sharing one with other detainees. Fewer witnesses to silence.

This surely wasn't the first time a hit had been placed on someone in this precinct by this unknown figure. And *that* suggested he was dealing with someone with the right people in his pocket. Or someone who was seated pretty high up in the chain of command, maybe even beyond that. In Zero's experience, it was always the former, but he remained optimistic that he'd be able to expose a *Mononoke* that was chest deep in politics. For now, all he needed to do was wait.

He might as well check on how Detective Chavez was coming along while he passed the time.

Focusing his energy, he reached out to the squad room, outlines forming in the darkness behind his eyelids. He pictured the squad room, its shape forming in his mind's eye, the figures that milled about coming into view. Their outlines were all gray, all like chalk on a blackboard, walking around unaware of the person watching them. He searched carefully, trying to pick out the object of his thoughts. He stopped his sweep of the room and settled on an aura that stood out among the rest.

As opposed the dull gray of the other officers, Chavez's aura was bright orange (she was making progress). Seated at her desk, she looked like she was going over a case, most likely the one regarding Michael's death. She looked like she had just taken a power nap, taking a sip of coffee to stay awake. Zero took a moment to color her in and take in her appearance. She was certainly a very attractive woman.

Skin the color of caramel, eyes the deepest shade of brown he'd ever seen, full lips pressed into a thin line. Black hair that stopped at the base of her neck, framing her soft yet stern features. It was really a shame they had met the way they did tonight. She was someone who he hoped to eagerly call friend one day. Michael had even voiced his opinion that she would fit in all well with "someone like him."

Was that why he manipulated her aura when he saved her last night, even though it cost him his life? Whatever potential he must have seen in her had to have been significant for him to take such a risk. And Zero would nurture that hidden talent into something that would save not just her life, but the lives of many. He owed to Michael to see what he had started through to the end. Closer inspection saw that Chavez had stopped her typing and was looking, her aura flaring slightly.

She had sensed his presence; good.

He cut off the connection to avoid increasing her suspicions of him and waited, feeling another aura close in on him. The cops thought they'd stripped him of all his weapons, never considering his *body* as his deadliest weapon. He heard the footsteps approach his cell; both were heavy against the ground. Both were male, one smelling of tobacco and wearing boots, the other smelled like coffee and cheap cologne and wore standard issue footwear. The mechanics of the door unlocking echoed through the corridor.

"You got company, freak," the officer grunted. His "prisoner" walked inside, expression impassive, and took a seat on the far side of the cell. Zero opened his left eye by a slight fraction, taking in the appearance of his cellmate. He couldn't be any more obvious if he actually tried. Black denim jacket, white t-shirt, and dark blue jeans. Brownish blonde hair slicked back with the grease he smelled earlier, hollow cheek bones, pale skin, and sharp green eyes.

His small mouth pursed as he leaned against the metal bars, his gaze trained squarely on him. Thin, skeletal fingers, intertwined in a pyramid resting on air. He stretched his limbs, a series of pops made audible by the spacious atmosphere between them.

Zero loosened his shoulders and stood up, stretching his legs, his focus on the new arrival. He could tell that he had just felt out his aura to make certain he was a Hunter; he had done the same to determine if he was a *Mononoke*. They stood antipode to each other, challenging the other to make the first move. Somewhere in the corridor, a pipe was leaking; the *bloop, bloop* of water collecting in a puddle on the floor reaching them. Zero's heartbeat fell in rhythm with the sound.

Taking a fighting stance, he prepared to strike when the next drop of water fell.

That was, before the officer standing outside the cell drew his weapon, aiming solely for Zero; a *Mononoke's* aura flaring around him.

Well that was certainly unexpected, he thought with slight panic.

***

Renee was at her desk, sipping coffee while she sifted through the files on Michael Strauss; he'd been heavily involved in legal proceedings. She wanted to make sure there was nothing that could leak to the press that would tarnish his image. She didn't know Strauss well enough, but she could tell that he was a good man; a man she owed her life to. There seemed to be a growing list as of late, his name being joined by one other: Zero Ozawa.

The boy was in holding, meditating on everything that had transpired in the last five hours, give or take. Even knowing that, she felt like he was right next to her, his blue eyes drilling a hole into her. It was the same thing she felt in the interrogation room, like he was reaching inside her, searching for something. She shuddered, wondering what he might have found, if anything at all.

That was until a gunshot thundered through the building, originating from the holding cells.

Every officer in the squad room was instantly aware of their surroundings, hands reaching for their guns. Renee was out of her seat first and tearing a path for holding, at least a dozen or more officers flanking her. She stopped just outside of holding, weapon in hand, steeling her resolve. Glancing back at the small group of officers behind her, she gestured for them wait while she checked things out. They nodded, holding their guns close to their chests, most of them were rookies, nervous at the prospect of their first kill.

Renee reached for the knob to enter holding when the door was pushed open, three shapes falling to the ground. The first shape, Zero Ozawa, quickly regained a vertical base and struck an offensive stance. The minute he did so, every officer present trained their guns on him, much to his chagrin.

"W-Wait!" he put his hands up in complacence. "I-I didn't do anything" He pointed at the two shapes on the ground, still trying to regain their footing. "*They* attacked *me!*"

The second shape gathered himself first, an officer with a round belly—sweat stains under his armpits from exertion—breaths ragged, stood up. He snarled at the boy, eyes burning with an intense anger, "He's lying! The second I opened the cell, he jumped me! You can't trust him! Shoot him! Now!"

"Oh come on!" he looked directly at Renee. "*You're* not buying this, are you? Why would I suddenly, out of nowhere, attack an officer?"

"He attacked Chavez in interrogation!"

"I didn't hurt her!"

"You might have hypnotized her into being your slave!"

"That a load of bull—"

"Both of you!" Renee roared, temples throbbing in annoyance, "Shut. The Hell. Up!" Both officer and the teenager promptly did as told, acting like scared little puppies. However, third party involved took the opportunity to attack Ozawa, who reacted too late, the former's first colliding with the latter's jaw. Recoiling backward, he was unable to defend against the knee to the stomach that sent him into a wall. Now he was under the scrutiny of the officers.

"Don't fire!" the officer tried to placate them. "I brought him on a DUI, but he was sober enough to help me keep that lunatic at bay."

Planting himself firmly in their line of fire, Chavez made note of something irregular, but was too distracted by the fight going in front of her. Ozawa managed to fight his way out of the corner and drive his attacker back. He blocked each strike and turned his momentum on him, throwing him across the small space. He recovered just in time for Ozawa to leap in the air, twirling, his right leg shooting outward. His foot connected with the attacker's chest, sending him reeling back into the Holding Cells.

***

Zero's would-be assassin fell to the ground, staring up at him, rage burning in his green eyes. He backed away from the Hunter and searched frantically for something to defend himself with. Seeing nothing, he settled for attacking like a wild animal; an animal with *skills*, mind you. He threw punch after punch at Zero, failing to the mark each time. When he tried for a kick, the Hunter caught his leg, ducked under it while clipping the other leg, and kneed him in the face when he was on his knees. The sickening crunch beneath his skin was heard, blood sputtering out of control.

"Who sent you?" he demanded.

"F-Fuck you," he gasped out, holding his nose. He made one final attempt before Zero rammed his fist through his chest cavity. He watched the Hunter helplessly before backing away, meeting the wall and sliding down into a sitting position. He stared into the distance as his eyes glazed over. He breathed heavily as the doors opened, Detective Chavez leading several officers inside. Glancing at the body, she glared at the masked boy before holstering her weapon.

Zero took a deep breath, the adrenaline starting to fade and pain setting in.

"I'm... pretty sure.. *that*," he gestured to the body, "counts as self-defense."

"Who the hell did you piss off?" she asked.

"That is a *long* list, Detective. How did you know the officer was lying? I mean, other than your instinct telling you I was right?" Chavez simply stared at him for a moment, then nodded her head toward the cell he'd been occupying. Huffing childishly, he complied and entered, the door shutting behind him. The other officers left the room. Chavez was the last to leave, sparing a glance at Zero.

"Because Officer Simon C. Ribe is dead."

Chapter 14

It had been decided it was better to let Captain Braddock rest than to wake him up with news that a fight had broken out between two detainees. He was already drained from a hard day's work at the precinct, made no easier by the arrival of Zero Ozawa. Sure, the captain would be furious to learn that he had not been called immediately following the altercation (especially once he heard that one of the detainees was dead) but at least he would be fully awake and prepared to deal with it all.

Of course, the rest of the squad had only agreed once Renee Chavez promised to take full responsibility for it all. It made sense to them; presumably, the fight had only happened because of Zero Ozawa. And who was the detective responsible for Ozawa being here? Thus it was only right that Chavez be the one to take responsibility.

Bunch of cowards, she thought to herself while she brought the captain up to speed.

"Where's our imposter now?" he asked in lieu of the expected display of anger. They were standing by the coffee maker, ignoring the squad as the pretended not to listen in. Honestly, there were days (and nights) where she felt like this was an elementary school classroom. The children eagerly watching as the singled out student was supposed to be in trouble with the teacher.

"In holding," she took a sip of coffee. "Said he'd tell us everything if we kept him away from Ozawa. Whoever this kid is, he seems to have quite the reputation."

"Maybe we're looking at this wrong, then," the captain rubbed his chin, a salt and pepper stubble beginning to form. "Instead of criminal record, we should be looking into any acts of vigilantism involving anyone matching his description. A kid wearing a skull mask would be impossible to miss."

"Hyde thought of that," she replied. "We couldn't find anything substantial. He's extremely careful. Also, the way he fights; he wasn't trained by some back-alley dojo. I'd say he's on a regimen similar to a soldier. At best."

With a nod, Braddock finished his coffee, ready to interrogate the imposter. Chavez sent an officer to fetch the impersonator and send him to his fate. She almost felt bad for him, having to face Thom Braddock after being caught impersonating a police officer.

Almost.

Returning to her desk, where Hyde, stationed to her left, just finished compiling a file on Ozawa. The kid was an enigma; the only person who may have known anything about him—Michael Strauss—was dead, but she wondered just how much Ozawa divulged to the reverend. Not to mention how much he allowed Strauss to share with anyone; she thought back to last night. If Strauss had been meeting with Ozawa, had it been to get permission to let her in on the secret? He claimed to have been too late to help Strauss, but without a witness for corroboration, it was just his word.

And she wasn't about to take that at face (mask) value.

"He said the reverend called him," she replied. "Ozawa. He said Michael Strauss wanted to meet with at the bar where he'd been killed."

"About you?"

"We under the assumption that someone didn't want the meeting between Strauss and myself to take place, right? Maybe Ozawa didn't want us discovering what kind of business he was up to. Back in interrogation, he slipped up and let out a word that had him panicked."

"Right? It was... Monopoly? Mono?"

"*Mononoke.* He said *a Mononoke* was responsible for the killings. Some kind of new gang? Nathan Vegan and Bruce Raymond couldn't have been the only ones hungry enough to take on Alex Roan."

Who are you trying to kid? a voice in the back in the back of her mind screamed. *You know exactly what the kids talking about. You're just too afraid to admit it. It's easier to deny what you saw instead facing, right?*

She ordered that part of her mind to shut up and focus on what was important. She had a killer or killers to catch. The last thing she needed was to start questioning herself on what was real and what wasn't.

"Makes sense," Hyde agreed. "What about the guy he iced last night, what did he have to do with any of this?"

"Some churchgoer who found out what happened and wanted payback?" the irrational part of her mind laughed the explanation away. "All I know is if we can connect these cases, we might be able to stop another slaying before it happens."

"Assuming O'Mara doesn't beat us to the punch."

"If he was that good, Bruce Raymond and company would still be alive. Any detective who chooses to work alone does it for two reasons: their first partner didn't watch their back and they paid for it, or they don't want to share the spotlight for major arrests with anyone else."

"Who's to say it's not both?"

Chavez had considered the possibility, but dismissed it all the same. Marcus O'Mara carried an air around him that screamed "hot-shot-lone-ranger". But there was something else about him; something she sensed after Ozawa had done whatever it was he did to her. It was as if there was more to O'Mara than she realized, a secret he was withholding.

Chavez knew she was the last person to cast stones over keeping secrets, but that self-confession did little to curb her suspicions.

"Detective Chavez," a voice from behind beckoned her.

The District Attorney, Duane Pierce, leaned against her desk. Hands in the pockets of dark blue pants, he looked a bit too relaxed for someone of his position and workload. Pierce was a dark-skinned man; his Native-American heritage made evident by the tribal necklace he wore around his neck. It was inherited from his great-grandfather, he had told them once, and was meant to ward off evil spirits.

"Busy morning?" he asked with a smile.

"You don't know the half of it," Hyde answered from his desk. "We've got a serial murderer, a dead reverend, and some crazy teen in a mask claiming that Monolithics are responsible. And before you ask, counselor, yes, he's sixteen."

"My lucky number," he checked his watch. "I take it this was the case Braddock was having a hard time deciding on? He also mentioned something about him killing two people."

"I was there and saw it myself," Chavez looked at him from her seat. "But the bodies are gone."

"And he was apparently rescuing Chavez, here." Hyde added. "So if your office decides to charge him with murder, whatever lawyer he can afford will make us out to be ungrateful pigs."

"Not to mention the media," Pierce tapped his chin thoughtfully. "I assume there's more."

"Last night, someone snuck in here and tried to kill him, but he fought them off and killed them."

"In self-defense, you mean?" his brow creased. "Not good. Any half-baked attorney fresh out of law school would argue negligence on the part of the police and have him released pending any potential trial. Anything else?"

"We may have evidence linking him to the murder of Michael Strauss, the reverend Hyde mentioned. Strauss was apparently allowing him to stay in a spare room at the church. We think he might have been upset when he learned Strauss was planning to contact the police about something."

"I've heard enough. Time to speak with this young man myself."

Chavez and Hyde retrieved Zero Ozawa from holding and led him to the interrogation room where Pierce was waiting. Along the way, the crossed paths with the impersonator of Simon C. Ribe and were treated to an interesting sight. Upon seeing Ozawa, he recoiled in fear and nearly dragged the officer escorting him into the wall with them.

"Keep him away from me!"

"Calm down," one of the officers snapped. "What the hell is guy on?"

"Same thing he's on," Chavez gestured to Ozawa, who beamed behind his mask in return. When they arrived at interrogation and sat him down in front of Pierce, the attorney took in the boy's appearance with a frown. Renee thought she saw his eyes sparkle with something before they settled into professionalism. She could also feel the pressure in the room increase, like the two of them being so close together in this enclosed space was going to tear it apart.

It made her head throb; she'd been fighting off a migraine since last night, but it was starting to fight back. Hyde insisted that she lay down for a spell and get some rest, but she said, "I'll rest when this is over."

D.A. Pierce took a look at the file on the table and nodded. He'd reached his decision.

"Mr. Ozawa," he looked him square in the eye. "You're free to go. On behalf of the District Attorney's office, you have my deepest apologies for the inconvenience."

Chapter 15

Both Chavez and Hyde simply stood there, watching, mouths agape, as D.A. Duane Pierce dismissed Zero Ozawa with another "apology" before. Nodding, the teen paid both detectives no mind as he reached across the table and shook Pierce's hand. He spared a glance at Chavez before locking eyes with Pierce once more.

"I'll need my weapons," he said plainly.

"They'll be returned to you immediately," the District Attorney assured. "You know the way out, I'm sure. Have a nice day."

"You as well," with a flick of his wrists, he rid himself of the handcuffs. Opening the door, he walked out of interrogation, followed by D.A. Pierce. For the longest time, neither Renee nor Jackson could say anything, could fathom what had just happened. Pierce, known for his staunch opposition to crime in New Orleans, who swore an oath upon taking office that he would try any and all cases to the best of his ability, had just let a suspect go, free of all charges.

"Did that just happen?" Hyde asked.

"What. The. Hell?" Chavez growled, storming out of the small room, Hyde to her left, after Pierce. When they reached the squad room, they caught the barest glimpse of Duane Pierce walking into the captain's office. Normally, they would leave the chewing out over bullshit decisions to Braddock, but last forty-eight hours hadn't left either in the mood to play it safe.

Hyde none too kindly swung the door open.

"What the hell was that?!" Chavez practically shouted, the door slamming shut behind them. "You just let him go without a word to us! Just who is that kid screwing to get that kind of treatment?"

"I was wondering the same thing," Braddock intoned, leveling the D.A. with the coldest of glares. "There's some teen in a mask, probably high up on some kind of narcotic and not *only* do you let him walk without even consulting me, you give him back a weapon Chavez here saw him use to cut up two people. You better have a damn good explanation counselor."

Amidst the glares and shouting, Pierce's expression never wavered; he adjusted his crimson tie, meeting their fury with serenity. His eyes roamed over each of them all briefly, settling on Chavez for a moment before facing Braddock. Standing up to his full height, Duane Pierce calmly reached into his suit and pulled out a file.

"I intercepted an officer bringing this to you. The lab report is back; the weapon didn't match any open homicides in our area, and didn't match up with the wounds on Michael Strauss's body. He didn't kill him."

"Not with *that* sword," Chavez argued. "Who's to say he doesn't have another one lying around somewhere? Heck, he's probably got a damn whole armory stashed away. Even if he didn't kill Strauss, *I* saw him butcher two people—"

"Who, if I'm not mistaken, were going to kill you, correct?" he inquired with a tone usually reserved for the courts. "Not to mention we have no bodies, so unless a blood test has come back identifying them, we've got nothing. I can't imagine many juries out there who'd want to convict a man for saving a cop, do you?"

Gathering his suitcase, he moved past the detectives and left Braddock's office, as well as the squad room.

Chavez, anger at the last two days' events reaching its zenith, followed him to the elevators. The occupants inside decided then to wait for another car, leaving the two of them alone. As soon as the doors closed shut, the detective hissed, "What's he got on you?"

"Beg pardon?"

"What's Ozawa got on you?" she asked again. "We've brought you cases with everything ranging from 'hardly any physical evidence' to 'circumstantial' and so on. You've gotten convictions, made headlines, given victims' families closure. It doesn't take a genius to assume that you only let Ozawa go because he's got something on you."

"What could he possibly have to blackmail me with?" Pierce raised an eyebrow. "I've never met him before today."

"Don't feed me that crap, I saw the way you looked at him as soon as we sat him down. You recognized him."

"Funny," he glared at her. "Your partner didn't seem to catch this supposed slip-up. How did you?"

"I'm good at reading people."

"But you've never had to 'read' me before, have you? A little convenient that you would think that I was off my game today. I've had to let plenty of suspects go because of lack of evidence and no one's ever called me out for 'recognizing' them." He shook his head at her, "Honestly detective, I think you need to get some sleep."

She clenched her hands into fists; it was all she could do not to punch Pierce in his face. She'd seen him take on a case where the defense had managed to build up enough reasonable doubt for the jury to either acquit or deadlock. Throughout the entire trial, the District Attorney never lost his composure. And, miraculously enough, he'd gotten a conviction against all odds. She still remembered the defendant shouting and cursing at him while he was being dragged away.

She actually *admired* this man and everything he stood for; now she had just seen him let a suspect go. Not only that, but he was talking down to her like she was some child! Chavez could feel her blood boiling, jaw clenching, temples throbbing. She was ready to punch a hole in the elevator before they reopened on her squad's floor. Then, she started to feel strange, like her entire body was engulfed in flames.

Everything within range of her vision started swaying back and forth, becoming blurred and unreadable. Chavez blinked a few times before risking a step out of the elevator. That proved to be a fatal mistake when her legs gave out under her and she collapsed on to the floor—on her injured side, no less`. Before she realized it, there were numerous shapes and shadows surrounding her, all talking at once. Darkness clawed at the edge of her vision, and she felt herself being lifted into the air.

Sneaking out of a hospital was something Renee had learn to do as a child, ever since her father's passing. She had the sterile and stoic environment that made up the facilities. The seemingly uncaring reality that promised death would always be somewhere around the corner. For every successful birth, there was, in all likelihood, an equally unsuccessful attempt to save a life. Thoughts like that never usually made their way into Renee's mind.

Except where hospitals were concerned.

Setting aside her discomfort, she set her mind to the task at hand: getting home and making sure Alex Roan didn't get to her husband, Ricardo. Waving a taxi, she got in, have him the address and sat back and let the city go by. To keep her worry from driving her mad, she thought back to how she'd first met Ricardo.

While in college, she and her friends went out to a bar to celebrate Renee making it into the police academy. She wasn't stupid enough to get drunk and risk an offense that would ruin an otherwise bright future. That didn't stop her friends from downing a few shots and celebrating in a way only they *could. It didn't take long before Renee realized she was being stared at by some guy in the corner of the bar. Rather than risk scaring him off, she used the cleanest spoon she could find and looked into the reflection.*

There he was, in the back corner, image distorted by the utensil, but she knew it was him nonetheless.

Perhaps it had only been the beer, but she was feeling brave and left her friends to their drinking to spark up a conversation. He glanced away from her, unaware that she'd already taken notice of him. Black hair thinned into a buzz cut, a clean shave that revealed a well-crafted jaw, soft lips, and a model's nose (if that made sense to anyone other than her). His green eyes flicked back to her and he realized that she was looking at him. She saw him blush when he deduced that he'd been caught staring, bringing a well-muscled arm up to rub the back of his head nervously.

The gray shirt he wore looked like it was struggling to keep his torso covered, she noted at the time.

"A little sad to be drinking alone," she said.

"Maybe I'm not celebrating like you and your friends are," he replied. "A bar's more than just a place for celebrations, you know?" Before she could think of anything to say, he continued: "I'm here for a buddy of mine, this was his favorite place to be when he wasn't working. Always drank in moderation. I never thought it was possible."

"I'm sorry."

"For what?"

"You friend. You mention him in past tense, means he likely... I'm just really sorry."

"Thanks," he smiled at her.

"I'm Renee Chavez."

"Ricky Kaplan. Call me Ricardo."

They chatted for the rest of the night, only parting when she realized her friends had elected her the designated driver. After exchanging phone numbers, they spoke almost every day after that. No matter what it was about, they talked for hours on end.

"You wanna go out?" he asked her over the phone one day.

Without giving it much thought, she agreed and they went out to dinner the next night. The following weekend, it was a movie; after that, a theatre show, then a night in the park. Before she knew it, they had been going out for six months. It had gotten harder thanks to the police academy, but they made it work. Then, during a holiday, it happened out of the blue.

They'd been having one of their usual dates when out nowhere, a simple kiss, turned into something much more. When it was over, Renee didn't really know how to feel about such a drastic change in their relationship. One thing she knew for sure: she didn't regret it. And he didn't either, given how gently he'd held her that night and all others after.

After about two years of dating, he finally proposed and again she have no thought before answering.

"Yes," she said, eyes burning with tears.

Four years into their marriage and Renee felt like they were in a good place in their lives. Smiling unconsciously, she glanced at her reflection in the window glass. The swelling in her right eye was going down and she could see a little better. Her body still ached with every bump the taxi made. The bruising where she'd been hit on the head was starting to change color, a sickly purple taking form there.

When she finally noticed they came to a stop outside the house she and Ricardo shared, she paid the driver his fee, plus an additional to stay in case they needed to get away without their cars. Getting out of the taxi, she arrived at her doorstep and reached into her pockets. It was then, that she remembered that she left her keys here so as not do draw suspicion from Roan (and look where that had gotten her). After a brief panic attack, her mind's light bulb clicked on and she checked under the welcome mat. There was a piece of stone that was loosened from the others, making it the perfect hiding spot for a key.

Unlocking the door, she opened it, flipping the light switch just as Ricardo stepped into the kitchen, Champaign bottle in hand. He was wearing nothing but underwear (nothing surprising about that). He looked shocked to see her; it was natural considering she'd been undercover for the last few months and probably looked like hell. Despite that, she was happy to see him and was about to hug him when she heard:

"Ricky," a distinctly feminine voice purred from the bedroom—their bedroom—and out stepped Mary Beckett, her friend since high school, all throughout college, and Maid of Honor at her wedding. She was wearing one of Ricardo's shirts loosely around her shoulders and waist, nothing else below. She eyed him with a lustful expression before following his gaze to Renee. Her eyes widened and her jaw failed her, her beautiful expression morphing into a dead-in-the-headlights one.

Chavez regained consciousness just as a pair of arms lifted her out of a car and carried her toward her house. She was still swimming in a sea of deliria, but could make out her home, but not the person carrying her. She felt a wave of panic before the shadow assured her everything was fine.

"H-Hyde . . . ?"

"Have a nice dream?"

"What—" she groaned when her injured ribs started to ache, the dizziness getting worse. Closing her eyes, she tried to fight the intruding discomfort, but it was a losing battle. She felt Hyde come to a stop. Opening her eyes briefly, she saw her front door and glanced at Hyde. She managed a mirthless grin, "I'd give you a tour, but . . ."

"Save it for the next time, I'm sure Martin would like it. He's been pressuring me to introduce him to you."

"It's a date, then."

"Can you reach for your keys?"

She fished them out of her pockets and handed them to Hyde, "First one to the left of little bear."

"It's cute."

"My dad made it for me."

Hyde unlocked the door and carried her inside and set her gently down on the sofa, a pillow under her head. He rested the back of his hand on her forehead, brow creasing in concern.

"What's wrong?"

"You passed out at the precinct," he explained. "You've got a pretty high fever, but nothing worth going to a hospital for. At least, I hope not." He disappeared from view for a few moments, followed by the sound of rushing water, before returning with a small towel. When he placed it on her forehead, she exhaled softly at the cold touch of the cloth. Hyde smiled before checking his cell phone.

"Go," she insisted. "I'll be fine. Just have Kira Massey next door check up on me."

"I'll have her call me if anything happens. But I'm not worried, you're too stubborn to let a fever keep you down for long. Take care, Renee." He patted her shoulder gently before leaving, locking the door behind him. Safe from public view, Chavez was free to groan in agony as much as she wanted. Whatever this was, it was no ordinary fever; she briefly entertained the idea that she was dying. Her entire body felt like it was on fire, the cool touch of the cloth quickly erased.

She closed her eyes tightly, everything around her spinning out of control.

"I thought he'd never leave."

Through the haze of discomfort and delirium, she recognized that voice, and her eyes were wide open now. Against the ever-changing shapes and shadows that used to be her home, she could make out one clear figure standing a few feet from her. She reached for her weapon, but she couldn't find it in this state.

Zero Ozawa advanced on her slowly; he was like a predator hungrily eyeing his prey.

She tried to cry out for help when his gloved hand, a skeletal pattern around it, reached for her. No such sound escaped her throat; only a strained moan barely audible to even her. His blue eyes watched her with an expression she couldn't make out, something hidden behind their shining gaze.

"Don't worry, Detective," he placed his palm on her forehead in a comforting gesture. "There's nothing to worry about, just sleep."

Chapter 16

Renee's eyes fluttered open, adjusting to the light of her ceiling fan, spinning a cool breeze onto her. Her body no longer felt as though it was on fire. In fact, she felt better than she had in the last two days, having been allowed to rest properly as opposed to a quick nap in an uncomfortable space. Sitting up, muscles stretching in response, Renee swung her legs over the couch. Hanging her head for a moment, she tried to remember what happened in the moments before she lost consciousness. She remembered panicking as someone approached her in such a weakened state.

Someone in a... skull mask!

The revelation was enough of a jolt for her body to wake up from its delirium and nearly jump to her feet. Zero Ozawa had been in her home, had been granted full access to her person while she was out cold, and, last she remembered, reached out towards her when her vision went black. She began a rigorous self-inspection, checking for anything out of place; mismatched buttons, stains of any kind, some kind of scent. By all counts, nothing had been done to her while she slept. That small comfort did nothing for the anger swelling up inside of her.

This all started back in the interrogation room, with Ozawa and his talk of Mono-whatever the hell he called it. Now, he'd been inside of her house, violated the one place that was supposed to be her escape from the job. There would be hell to pay, and she was intent on collecting it soon.

"Ah, you're awake."

Renee looked towards her kitchen and found she was being greeted by the object of her fury. Zero Ozawa appeared to have just finished prepping meal on her counter, steam rising from a plate of Sizzling Chicken and Linguini covered in a white-wine sauce. Next to the plate was a glass of green, murky-looking, water, and some bread. In all honesty, the very sight of it made her stomach growl in hunger. Barely, she resisted the urge to eat before questioning the intruder in her home.

"You've got some balls," she sneered. "Breaking into a cop's house, taking advantage of a woman while she's unconscious. What the hell are you doing here, Ozawa?"

"Making you a nice Italian meal, Detective," he finished turning a small napkin into a swan via *Origami*. He turned to face her, offering a comforting smile, "As for the 'taking advantage of' part, I did no such thing, I'll have you know. I'm a gentleman."

"Who breaks into people's houses."

"And cooks them a nice meal. But that's beside the point. Right now, you need to something, so dig in."

He offered her a knife and fork, trying to look as harmless as someone of his appearance could be. She eyed him with a distrustful, suspicious, gaze while standing firmly in the spot by the coach. He was clearly getting annoyed with her reluctance, and moved forward slightly, stopping when he noticed her reach of her gun. She found nothing at her waist and glanced around the room, providing Ozawa with enough time to invade her personal space and grasp her hands. Her eyes snapped back to his and glared at him, "Let me go."

"Will you eat?" he asked.

"Do I look stupid to you?"

"You look hungry."

Her traitorous stomach growled in agreement with his assessment, her cheeks flushing a slight pink. The masked boy grinned triumphantly and stepped back, holding the knife and fork out for her to grab. Stubbornly, she refused to take them, instead inquiring: "For all I know, you could have poisoned the food, that drink, or the utensils."

He rolled his eyes, "You've seen me; you know what I'm capable of. I don't need poisons to kill you. I just want you to eat so you can get your strength back. You're no good to anyone like this."

"Screw you."

"There will be time for that later," he grinned cheekily at her. Renee looked behind her, saw her weapon lying on the table, and moved to pick it up. Ozawa panicked and added, "I was only kidding! I promise you, Detective, I didn't poison the food. Here," he approached the plate and stuck the fork in the chicken and wrapped it in linguini. With his back to her, he pulled down his mask and placed the food in his mouth, "See? Nothing?"

He swallowed and offered her the knife and fork once again. Sighing, she stepped around him and pulled out a new fork and took the knife. Eyeing the food suspiciously one more time (while sparing a glance at Ozawa), she started eating. The second she tasted the food, she was struck by a flavor and sensation she'd never quite felt before. She wolfed down the meal greedily and sent the strange drink after it.

Seeing Ozawa grinning behind his replaced mask, she blushed again, doing her best to act as professional as poosible. So the meal was apparently the genuine article, that didn't excuse the fact that he broke into her house. Neither did it explain everything that had been going on since she first met him outside *Celui Qui Réfléchit*. She wasn't prone to fainting spells or fevers that came out of nowhere, not to mention the sensations she had been feeling back at the station. The feeling that he'd been reaching into her personal space without actually being near her.

"At the station," she began. "You slipped up. Said something you clearly didn't want me to hear. What are *Mononoke?*"

"I didn't mean to keep it a secret since you've been brought into the loop," he answered. "I just wasn't supposed to tell you at the station. I can be a bit of air head sometimes—"

"No argument there," she interjected.

"—and forgot that the worlds of men and spirit aren't meant to collide just yet. My clan and I refer to them as '*Mononoke*', but a more colloquial term used around the world would be 'spirits.' They are creatures that can pass themselves off as humans, but are in reality anything but. Much like Alex Roan, as you learned last night. What you saw was no hallucination, but his true form."

She considered his words for a brief moment, finding some sense in them, and began replaying the events of that night. She realized it couldn't have been a hallucination; Michael Strauss had been there, he'd *seen* Roan's "true form." She couldn't have imagined him there, especially since he showed up dead the next day. Drugs were also ruled out; the doctors would have found something in her system (unless it already metabolized by then, the rational part of her mind tried to reason). Which meant what she saw last night—the three punks who'd changed into beasts—was real despite her every instinct telling her otherwise.

"I guess this is the part of the film where I say, 'The world as you know it has ceased to exist.'" He offered her a formal bow and smiled at her through his mask, eyes tightened into joyful slights.

"Welcome to my nightmare."

Chapter 17

Renee Chavez sat on her coach, watching Zero Ozawa as he cleaned the plate and utensils in her sink. He hummed an unfamiliar melody, swaying back and forth in rhythm with the tune, and seemed unbothered by her staring. Unbothered by the fact that the world, as she knew it, was inhabited by spirits from some alternate plain of existence. Then again, according to him, he and his ancestors were keenly aware of this bizarre truth. She couldn't think of anything to say that would make this matter any more sensible.

What could she say?

"How long have these things been here? The *Mononoke*?"

"For about as long as we've been here. They veil between the two worlds has always been thin. It's a long and complicated history; one I'd be more than willing to share if we had the time."

"You said Strauss did something to me when he brought me home," she said.

Zero finished cleaning her dishes and entered the living room. It was only then that she realized he was dressed differently than he had been last night, sans his mask. Gone was the black combat suit used in dispatching the demons last night; in its place, a black Japanese school uniform, button shirt hanging open to reveal a red undershirt, black gloves over his hands, and white tennis shoes.

He sat in the armchair to the right of the coach, arms resting on the armrests, right leg crossed over the left, eyes searching an invisible data log.

"I can sense the *Mononoke* around me by feeling their aura," he explained. "If I had to pick, I'd say it's kind of like the 'Force.' I can feel the life around me, can sense the energy of the animals, the trees, and the people. By focusing on a particular point, I can locate abnormalities in certain people's aura. The 'dark side', if you will. With it, I can see *Mononoke* for what they truly are.

"It's the same if I'm trying to find a person with an acute spiritual aura, or a budding one like yours. When I search for the energy, it presents itself as a certain color, depending on how far along the person is. Last I checked, yours was a healthy baby blue. Which means your aura has accepted the change. Using his own aura, Michael heightened you aura's spiritual senses, but your body wasn't prepared for it. I added my own aura to ease the process along. I hadn't you would have been through more than just a fainting spell and a fever."

"You said my *body* wasn't prepared?"

"The ideal time to awaken someone's spiritual awareness is during infancy, preferably in the first year. Because our auras are at their most susceptible. During adulthood, you run the risk of death, more or less. Even though he knew this, Michael probably risked it so he could bring you into the fold."

"Fold?" she repeated suspiciously.

"Until today, it was just myself, Michael, and Pierce."

"Pierce? The District Attorney? Duane Pierce?"

'The very same," he chuckled, clearly finding amusement in her shock. "He couldn't risk being linked to me if this went to trial. Talk about a political nightmare. Besides, it would been controversial anyway, charging a guy for saving a cop."

"Moving on," she growled.

"Pierce didn't do much other than let us know which *Mononoke* to be on the lookout for. You see, there are as many of them here as there are people. They blend in with society, choosing only to meet in secret. For the most part, it's nothing worth getting excited over."

"But then there's the occasional trouble maker?" she guessed.

"You've seen Alex Roan," he snorted. "Unfortunately, not all the *Mononoke* are content with just living in peace. Some have often tried to spread pain and misery; either for sheer enjoyment, or because they have no choice."

"What do you mean?"

"For the most part, they're like animals, following only their base instincts," Zero explained. "Sometimes, they can't help the things they do, other times, the relish in it."

"So you don't kill every *Mononoke* you meet?"

He frowned at her, visibly affronted, "I'm guessing you know about Maurice, so no, I don't. Would *you* shoot an animal that was acting only instinct? Would kill it outright without seeing if there was another way? What I did last night was necessary, but I prefer to end things without confrontation."

"Point taken," she amended. "I'm still finding this whole thing hard to believe, but maybe a little demonstration might help."

He caught the note of a challenge in her tone, "What do you suggest?"

"You said you can sense *Mononoke*? Can you find out where they are? Like the one you think is responsible for the killings? Could you be able to locate them before they strike again?"

"Only if certain conditions were met," he replied. "Usually, their aura would have to be flaring before I can sense them. Their human skin acts like a shield. Like what happened at the station. Of course, that becomes a moot point if there's another, more powerful aura present as well."

She looked to the carpet again; of course it wouldn't be that easy. Things seldom were for her, but it was worth asking to know the limits of this newfound sense she had, apparently, been granted. So she couldn't find this thing if it was out there somewhere, slaughtering people because it either wanted to, or didn't have a choice.

"However," Zero continued, "I can find a *Mononoke* I've been in contact with in some form or another. Regardless if they're in human form. I could show you that."

She considered his offer for moment; it was better than nothing. "That punk from last night. The one who got away, could you find him?"

"I left my shuriken sticking out of his eye socket," he stood and began pushing her furniture out of the way. "Even if he removed it, there's enough of my aura for me to get a read on him," he patted the floor, sitting crossed-legged, "Come, sit."

Renee complied, crossing her own legs, and sitting directly across from him, mirroring his position. She still couldn't believe what he was telling her, but what she'd seen was real, there was no doubt about it. And since Strauss had gone to the trouble of "awakening" her, she owed to him to put it to use. Zero removed his gloves and held his hands out, palms open, waiting for her to take them. She laid her hands on his palms and waited for instructions.

"Close your eyes."

Taking a deep breath, she did.

"Keep your breath relaxed, heartbeat level, and mind clear of distractions."

Renee did as told and waited for whatever he was about to do; she felt it when it started. It was like a she was sitting on the surface level of an ocean, the waves gently rocking back and forth. She could vaguely feel another person's presence—Zero, she assumed—sitting in front of her. He was relaxed, having most likely done this many times before, his outline glowing the same color as pale moonlight. A moment later, it started to become unfocused.

"Concentrate," his voice echoed. "Don't focus on a singular point, you have to sense the entire world around you."

She followed his advice, and things became clear again.

This time she felt herself being elevated into the sky above her home, above New Orleans. The city's outline was a dull gray, betraying the excitement of the Big Easy. Though she didn't allow herself to become distracted, she admired the sensation she felt, as though she were looking at the city for the first time in her life, seeing it through the eyes of a child arriving to enjoy a vacation with their parents.

Suddenly, she felt herself being dragged into the city's interior, passing through buildings while scanning them for the intended target. It was like searching an internet browser for an address, millions of data bytes being checked against the original for a match. Was this what it felt like to be a computer? Renee wondered. The emotions she experienced were mix of wonder and dread; what if her mind was lost in this endless sea of energy? Just as abruptly as the search began, it ended, and she found herself watching the punk from last night.

His aura was a crimson flame, burning brightly and furiously, as he paced back and forth hurriedly. There was a flicker of moonlight silver (Zero's aura) located where his eye used to be. The shuriken was still implanted in his eye, she realized with slight discomfort; eyes were among the most sensitive parts of the human anatomy. Just picturing something like a throwing star stuck in there was enough to make most people cringe. The punk, however, didn't seem bothered by it.

"I'm gonna kill that bastard..." he growled. "He slaughtered them. My boys. *My boys!*"

She could feel the raw anger, the primal hatred, surging through him; the intense desire to find Zero and rip him to shreds. She was pretty sure that it was Zero's presence that kept her from being overtaken by these desires. Even so, she felt her heartbeat increase slightly, and she began to shake nervously. She could feel Zero's aura strengthen and envelope her like a coat. Renee appreciated the gesture, though she didn't voice it (she could tell he knew).

She felt another presence nearby; another *Mononoke.*

This one's aura was decidedly more introverted; either it was weaker or, more likely, it was better at concealing itself. Whatever it was, there was an energy that seemed almost familiar; like she knew the person it belonged to. But much of the energy seemed too foreign, and she couldn't place it. Renee settled for observing as the scene played out before her. The punk stopped his pacing to acknowledge the newcomer, his aura still blazing, but dimming slightly.

Beneath the intense fury, a new emotion flickered; if she didn't possess the instincts of a detective, Renee might have missed it. And she felt her stomach twist into a knot at the feeling, not sure how to process it.

Fear; the punk was afraid.

Given how fearsome he would seem to any normal person, Renee wasn't sure she wanted to meet whatever could make him afraid. The newcomer entered the room and examined the punk up and down. She felt a twinge of amusement as he chuckled; followed by the indignation radiating from the punk at not being taken seriously.

"'Bout fucking time you showed up," he hissed. "Why the hell didn't you tell that a goddamn *Hunter* was here?! He *killed* my boys!"

"But why not you?" a gurgling voice questioned. "Why are *you* still alive?"

"Because I got the hell outta dodge! I'm not dumb enough to take on a Hunter head on. Isn't that what you fucking Contractors are for? After all, you—"

"You *ran*," the voice whispered—making it sound all the more terrified. The aura around it began to surge, glowing a bright red.

"Detective," Zero's voice, filled with a calm urgency, reached her. "You have to end the connection, now!"

But she didn't listen, *wouldn't* listen; she was too immersed in what was playing out before her. Something inside of her told her she should heed Zero's warning, but she continued watching. She wondered to herself: *A Contractor? What is that?*

The punk tensed in fear and decided to strike first — assuming his *Mononoke* form — and leapt at his would-be aggressor. What followed next was, to say the least, the equivalent of being caught in jet turbine as it heated up. An explosion of energy that surged through her body, sending her from a sitting position to the floor. She was breathing heavily, chest heaving up and down, and realized she was back in her living room. Zero was staring down at her in a mixture of concern and amusement.

"Listen to me, next time, will you?"

Chapter 18

Chavez greedily downed a glass of water—her *ninth*—in order to quell the burning sensation in her throat. When the initial shock of what she'd seen finally wore off, her body started to itch and she found that she was sweating profusely. No matter how much water she drank, the burning wouldn't leave her; it didn't hurt too badly, but it was irritating as hell. But not as disturbing as witnessing a murder. Even though she'd seen her fair share of death in this line of work, nothing could describe what she felt the moment that punk had been killed.

At first, she hadn't been entirely sure what happened, but Zero had explained to her as she started downing glasses of water.

"I told you before, we were tapping into life energy," he had stated. "When we focus on specific target for an extended period of time, we can feel their emotions, can tell things about them that most people would miss. But that also makes us vulnerable to backlash of their death, or, more specifically, their murder. When someone dies of natural causes, such as old age or illness, the flame of life flickers out. When their life is ended suddenly and abruptly, the 'explosion' you experienced varies depending on the severity of the death."

She finished her tenth glass of water, "What about suicide?"

"That's a little tricky," the boy rubbed his chin, his expression thoughtful. "Things like pills and voluntarily hanging yourself are harder to decipher. But falling off a building or dropping a toaster in the tub are clearer cases. People still do that, right?"

"Can you tell if it was murder or suicide after the fact?"

"That'd be cheating, Detective," he reprimanded half-heartedly. "No, when someone dies, their life energy is released. No way to tell the cause. Very sorry."

Renee nodded and processed the information, her body finally cooling down; she felt like a computer server that had been overheated. It was still very disturbing, not only watching, but feeling someone's death. That wasa sense of intimacy she wasn't comfortable feeling, especially since it was with someone who'd tried to kill her. Deciding it was better not the think about it, she focused on the parts of the conversation that had intrigued her. She'd heard that gargling voice before.

It's dangerous to leave loose ends. Eventually, they come undone and everything falls apart.

That was what the voice had told Alex Roan at *Bête Noir* two nights ago, just before he attacked her. Was it possible that who or whatever that thing was, is responsible for the deaths of those men? She thought back to the hit man at the hospital, she'd only seen the back of his head, tan skin and a shaven head. Not much to go on, but at least it was something. Filing that information away, Renee thought about the other parts of the conversation.

What was it the punk had called his visitor turned killer? A "Contractor?"

"The *Mononoke*," she met Zero's gaze. "You said there's an entire plain of existence for them? Does that mean there are different types of them?"

"Yes," he confirmed. "Many, in fact. But I take it, you want to know more about the contractors. Parasitic-types, or 'Contrac-tors' as we call them, are born with a weakened constitution, they can't survive outside the spiritual plain for long. They need hosts to provide them with the necessary energy to keep them rooted here. Without them, their own supply of energy runs out and they wither away into nothing. In my experience, they usually take the forms of insects like—"

"Wasps," Renee finished. "How long can they survive on the host's energy?"

"Depends on the host," he crossed his arms. "As well as the energy they expend daily. Ideally, you want someone with an abundant amount of aura. When they run out, they have to move on two a new host quickly. However, Alex Roan found an exception to the rule. Most contractors only have one hosts, but they can have as many as possible. The reason they don't is because they're either taken or don't believe in what they're being promised. That's why the fact that Roan's been lingering here for so long seemed so confusing to me and Michael. Even with the most spiritually acute hosts, contractors usually drain them of energy in about a year."

"But you found something out?"

"Yes, even an aura that is dormant can fluctuate when . . ." he trailed off, tugging somewhat nervously at his mask. He averted his gaze from hers and stared at a wall like it was the most interesting thing in the world. She watched him patiently, wondering what made him so... flustered. Then, she noticed his ears burning red; he was blushing; it hit her like a water balloon.

"You've got to be kidding me," she gave him a deadpan look. "Are you saying that Roan is living off the energy 'fluctuated' by people having...? What kind of sick, perverted, jackass would—" She stopped when she remembered the second floor of *Bête Noir,* where she'd heard the moans and thrusts and slaps of skin. And Roan, whose office was at the end of the hall, as if nothing of the sort was going on just outside. He was bathing in the energy even as they were questioning him about Monique, when he pretended to actually be concerned about her. The sick bastard was getting off on laughing at them—at *her*—behind their backs.

Zero cleared his throat, "A-Anyway, as long as Roan provides the, um, 'mood', they'll keep giving him the energy he needs to remain intact without the risk of expending his own."

"Could he have shared this method with another Contractor?"

"Not likely, too much risk of competition stealing his power sources," Zero searched his internal database again. "But LeBlanc might be able to give us some info."

Renee nodded and reached into her pocket for her cellphone, just as it started buzzing. Checking the Caller ID, she frowned in confusion when the number read for the church where Strauss had served as Pastor. She answered the phone, "Chavez."

"Detective," a voice whispered.

"Who is this?"

"Reverend Strauss's secretary," she answered. "I need your help. Some thugs have broken into the church. I managed to lock myself in the Reverend's office, but I don't know how long it'll be until they find me. Please, you have to—" There was a crash that sounded like it came from the other room. "Hurry."

She hung up and Renee grabbed her gun and threw a coat on.

"What's wrong?" Zero asked, following her.

"Police business."

"I figured out that much," he persisted. "That was Alexis. She's supposed to be at the church this time of day. The only reason she'd call you is if something was wrong."

"Don't get involved," she snapped. "This isn't something"

"Someone's at the church, right?" he pressed. "If so, then they're there because of me. Word probably spread that I was here in New Orleans, and the *Mononoke* who think of me as an enemy have likely deduced where I've been staying. If that's the case, I'm going with you. My weapons are and if they fall into the wrong hands, it's not going to be pretty; and the longer you stand here arguing with me, the sooner Alexis will be found and hurt, or worse."

"You done?"

"For now."

"Then get in."

***

"This is Detective Chavez," she spoke into the phone while keeping her eyes on the road. "I need uniforms at the location I'm sending you. Be advised, there are multiple perpetrators and they are likely armed and dangerous. And they may have a hostage."

"Roger that," Dispatch responded and ended the call.

Renee and Zero got out of her car that had been parked just outside the church, rounding around to the trunk where the detective kept a bullet-proof vest. She handed it to Zero for protection (though he insisted it was unnecessary) and together, they slowly advanced on the building. Scouting the parking lot, she noticed a black SUV (no license plates) parked outside the rear entrance. That meant she could expect at least six men, potentially armed, and with a hostage.

Zero tapped her on the shoulder and gestured for her to follow, moving around to the front of the church. Taking charge, Chavez pushed open the double doors to the lobby, checking the corners and shadows before proceeding further. They entered the Sanctuary, the red carpet running down to the podium where

Strauss had held his weekly sermon. Three sections were occupied by rows of bleachers, screwed into the floor, red cushions in lieu of seats, and bibles on the back of each of them. The windows, glass-paintings depicting various images, colored the sunlight shining through them.

Once more, Chavez was struck by the feeling that she was committing a sort of taboo by bringing a weapon into this building. The feeling worsened when she realized that a possible shootout was imminent—they were always a possibility. It didn't help that they were in such an open space, vulnerable to being shot at from anywhere. She kept her hearing tuned for the sounds of sirens that would signal the arrival of back-up. With the Sanctuary apparently clear, they went into the hallway; there, they could hear the sounds coming from the Fellowship Hall.

There were two voices speaking; the closer they got, the more they could make out.

"Last chance," the first snarled. "Tell us where he is!"

"I-I t-told you," the second, Alexis, whimpered. "I don't know. He comes and goes, never bothers anyone so we leave him alone." A small shriek was heard before she started sobbing, Chavez and Zero just outside the door. Hugging the wall, she closed her eyes and tried to remember which way the door swung when opened.

"All six of them are in there," Zero said, eyes closed; he was feeling out there auras. "Two are by the door leading outside, one in the kitchen snacking, two more positioned on both sides of this door, and the last interrogating Alexis. Oddly enough, they're all human, so maybe a *Mononoke* sent guns for hire."

"We'll need to wait for back-up," Chavez said. "It's too risky to go in with them holding her hostage."

"They won't get here in time," the masked boy declared. "I'm the one they're after. The only way this ends is if I give them what they want."

"Not happening," she glared at him. "This isn't some John Wayne flick, where you can just go in guns blazing and hope everything turns out all right."

"You like John Wayne?"

"My dad did."

"I was more a Clint Eastwood guy myself. Of course, the western of his I've seen is *The Unforgiven*."

"Didn't everyone die in that movie?"

"I don't know. I hardly remember it. Besides, even without *Araguru-getsu-ga*, I still have a few tricks up my sleeve." Stepping in front of the door, he struck a stance and sucked in a deep breath of fresh air. Keeping his eyes closed, Zero Ozawa stood there, motionless, for several seconds, much to the confused annoyance of Chavez. As soon as he opened his eyes again, he placed his palm flat against the door and, almost immediately, reduced the door to splinters. The force of the blow drew the attention of those present in the Fellowship Hall.

Zero sprinted towards Alexis's captor and landed a solid punch on the bridge of his nose, knocking him to the ground, nose broken. Chavez tackled one of the guards by the door to the ground, while the other fumbled with the safety on his gun. When he switched it off, bullets sprayed everywhere, miraculously missing everyone. The two guarding the back door charged at Zero simultaneously, bringing their fists up. They seemed to have some formal training in martial arts, but the skull-masked teen was ready for them.

He blocked each of their punches with his elbows, ducking between them, and kicking one of them in the knee, a sickening crack heard. While their partner howled in pain, collapsing to the ground, the remaining three tried to take out Zero.

The one who fumbled with his weapon earlier trained the muzzle squarely on Zero, ready to fire when Chavez stopped him. Using her arm to force the gun downward, she slammed her elbow into his face, his head bouncing off the wall. She aimed for the one emerging from the kitchen, his gun apparently forgotten. He was smart enough to raise his hands in the air and get on the ground while she cuffed him. She tended to Alexis while Zero and the last remaining intruder did battle.

He managed to dodge a few of Zero's strikes, then went on the attack, grabbing the boy's arm and tossing him over the shoulder. However, as soon as he hit the floor, his left leg shot up and struck the intruder on the crown of his head. Back to his feet, Zero caught his punch and drove his elbow into the face of his opponent. Reeling back, Zero repeated the attack and sent him to the ground unconscious. The immediate danger over, he decided to interrogate one of the intruders; he glanced at the one with the broken knee.

Who better to start with?

When he noticed Zero's approach, the man tried to drag himself away, but failed when he felt a pressure on his injured leg. Hissing, he glared up at the Hunter in defiance, a string of curses passing through his lips. Instead of words, Zero crouched down, adding more weight to his foot (Oh, how his prisoner appreciated that) and searched the bulge in his coat pocket. He pulled out a small stone, staring intently at the kanji carved into it.

Bara; Rose.

In that moment, he felt overcome by an intense anger, clutching the stone with all his might, reducing it to a pile of small pebbles.

So *he* sent them?

Not surprising.

When the intruder tried to grasp at his clothes, hair, something for any kind of leverage, the masked teen promptly slammed his head into the tiled floor. Shuddering in anger, he struggled to regain control of himself before the detective noticed—if she hadn't already. Calming himself, he went to check on Alexis just as the wail of sirens was heard in the distance.

Chapter 19

Chavez watched Strauss's secretary, Alexis, a blanket draped over her shoulders as she sat in the ambulance, and Zero Ozawa as he gave a bogus statement while crossing his arms. If he noticed the cool scrutiny he was placed under by the other officers (which he did), he didn't seem bothered by it. Instead, he kept his focus on Alexis, concern clear in his eyes, partnered with the guilt of knowing the six men currently waiting in squad cars were here for him. She returned her attention to Captain Braddock, Hyde, and Marcus O'Mara, all watching her curiously. They obviously weren't buying her and Ozawa being here as a coincidence.

"Seems like trouble follows that kid wherever he goes," O'Mara observed with clinical disinterest. "And it seems like he follows *you* wherever you go, Chavez."

"He said Reverend Strauss lent him the spare bedroom," she paid O'Mara no mind. She trouble focusing though, thinking back to the Fellowship Hall, where there was sure to be an imprint of that goon's. That first time she'd seen the kid angry; he could give her a run for her money.

She didn't know what to make of it, so she didn't think about it.

The officers finished taking his statement and let Ozawa go; he immediately went to check on Alexis. Chavez felt it would have been better if she was there to moderate, so she met him halfway and they arrived at the back of the ambulance together. Her hair was a mess, eyes bugging out like white marbles with dark brown spots. She looked exactly like Monique did when they found her in the old theatre, her eyes focusing on the two people before her. She focused all of her attention on Zero, face contorting into a mixture of shock and rage.

"You..." she hissed, managing to convey the venom in the word as though it were a curse. A hateful fire burned in her eyes, body shaking with barely contained fury, and all of it was directed at the masked boy. The anger he'd let show earlier seemed to pale in comparison, his blue eyes widening in surprise and fear. Chavez didn't know what to say; she never did in these kinds of situations.

"Alexis—"

"He's dead because of *you!*" she shrieked. "Everything that's happened is all *your* fault!"

Zero looked ready to try and offer an explanation when she suddenly exploded out of the ambulance and tackled him to ground. She knew it was only out of surprise that Zero allowed her to do so, otherwise he would have easily stepped aside. Alexis straddled him, hands fisting his red shirt, breaths hissing between her teeth. Chavez wondered if her body couldn't decide which emotion—anger or despair—was safer to cling on to. She settled for beating on his chest, the impact appearing to have no particular effect on him.

"Why?" she cried. "Why did he have to die? He was a good man! Why not you? It should have been *you!*"

The officers pulled Alexis to her feet and placed her back in the ambulance; she now resembled a hollowed out doll. The effect of near-death, the knowledge that you were this close to dying only to be rescued, it often summoned forth a tidal wave of emotions. In Alexis's case, anger directed at Zero Ozawa was the first to break through, never mind the fact that he'd saved her life.

The officers present watched as Ozawa pulled himself to his feet and left the parking lot, only Chavez could catch flicker of hurt in his eyes. The guilt at knowing he had been responsible for the death of Michael Strauss, that he had nearly gotten Alexis killed, and whatever else he carried with him. But the detective knew it wasn't fair; she had been just as responsible for the pastor's death. She felt a desire to go after him, if only to make sure he would be safe. Right now, she didn't see that enigmatic young man in the mask, who smiled away the glares and accusations.

He was just a kid who'd likely been through more than his fair share of emotional trauma. Part reasoned that he'd survived this long; he'd keep going until they rendezvoused to meet LeBlanc.

"You think these guys have anything to do with Strauss's murder?" she asked the three men before her. "If they knew Ozawa was here, they either learned it from Strauss or were sent to take them both out. Might explain why someone went to the trouble of sending two hired guns into the precinct to kill him last night."

Hyde shrugged, "Makes sense. I could buy this kid making a few enemies given his tendency to go all Rambo with that sword. But who has enough time and money to devote to getting rid of two people?"

"Alex Roan," O'Mara offered. "I recognize all six of them. Low-level members of his gang that doesn't work out of *Bête Noir*."

"This was too sloppy for Roan," Braddock countered. "Too many guys, in a church of all places, not to mention unnecessary collateral damage with the secretary. And the fact that there's a connection to Roan at all makes it obvious someone wants us to think it was him."

"What are the odds our masked friend knows who it is?" O'Mara asked, searching the area for any sign of him. The detective had to admit, when the kid wanted to disappear, he left no traces. But they'd find him eventually; his instinct told him that this wouldn't be the last time Ozawa interfered in the case. Unless he managed to put a stop to these killings here and now.

***

Chavez and Hyde watched Matthew Owens, the apparent leader of the gang that stormed the church, the one who'd gotten his nose bashed into his face by Ozawa, bandage present. He sported several bruises, the reddening skin camouflaged by his dark, wrinkled, complexion. Beneath his snow cap, thinning, graying, black hair exposed his scalp, green eyes burning a hole through the two-way mirror. He'd done nothing except stare at his reflection in the two-way mirror since he was brought in, not even demand a lawyer. Just sat there, waiting for something to happen.

"One of Roan's thugs," Hyde observed. "Two collars for assault, one of them was a domestic. Both times, the victim spent the night in the hospital. What's that tell you?"

"That he's more 'hands on' than the guy were looking for," Chavez checked the file. "Strauss was found with a gash from his shoulder to his hip. Marshall's report said it was a clean cut, the jagged lines found were from a serrated blade."

Hyde nodded, "You realize that that doesn't rule out Ozawa, right?"

"If that's the case," she tucked the file under her arm and headed for interrogation, "I'd hate to be Duane Pierce."

Once inside, the two detectives locked it behind them and pulled chairs to the small table that separated them and Owens. His eyes became focused again as he conveyed his barely concealed contempt for the two cops, snorting particularly in Chavez's direction. The expression he regarded them with said: *I've been through this before, you've got nothing to surprise me.*

"Good evening, Mr. Owens," Hyde began. "We understand that you've denied medical attention. That nose looks pretty bad. The doc's said you were hit with enough force to give a grown man a concussion."

"I barely feel a thing."

"You know," Chavez smiled sweetly at him. "I heard that if a concussion's bad enough and you fall asleep, you slip into a coma. Without any medics nearby, I can't imagine you'd be waking up any time soon. Now, are you certain you do not want medical attention?"

"So you can handcuff me a gurney? No thanks."

"Well, you did break into a church and take a woman hostage," she said in a matter-o-fact tone. The clenching of his jaw suggested he didn't like being spoken to in condescending fashion; even less so by a woman. She let her lips curl into a smirk, letting him know she caught on to his little insecurity, and that she'd exploit it. "I can guess you're probably not the smartest guy in the world, considering you dropped out of high school."

"Fuck you, bitch," he growled. "I graduated."

"Congratulations," she laced her voice with enough sugar to rot teeth. "You must have worked *so* hard."

Hyde tagged in, "Who told you Zero Ozawa was staying at the church?"

"Your girlfriend," he spat. "I enjoyed 'interrogating' her. Said I could do it any time I wanted."

"Good for you," he shared a knowing glance with Chavez. "I've always made it a priority to make sure she's satisfied. Did you know this man?" He slid a picture of Michael Strauss in front of Owens, who glanced away. "I'll take that as a yes."

132

"Okay, I made a confession," he shrugged. "That against the law now too? Or do you only interrogate religious *black* folks?"

Chavez rolled her eyes, "Really?"

Owens snorted and decided the wall to his right was more interesting than talking to the detectives. His entire form was rigid, meaning he was nervous; Chavez knew it had something to do with the *Mononoke* responsible for Strauss's death. Did *it* send them? The only person who could answer that was Zero, but she knew he needed a little more time. Shaking away the thought, she resumed her task of antagonizing him.

"I guess we shouldn't expect much from you," she got up and gathered the files. "You're so low on Roan's food chain that being asked to spit-shine his shoes is the most important thing you've ever done for him, right?"

"Kiss my ass."

"No, Roan's far too big to let a good-for-nothing like you anywhere near his ass. But that might explain why everything you're telling me smells like a load of crap. Let me tell you what happened: Roan, or someone else, sent you to kill Michael Strauss, adding insult to injury by not sending someone a little more competent."

"Shut up."

"You followed him to the bar—I'd say you lured him there, but that would have required you to possess an actual thought process."

Owens shot to his feet, "I said shut up, you bitch!"

"Somehow you managed to get him to the alley—probably the most brilliant thing you've ever thought of—and attacked him. You fought him to the kitchen, where pulled your gun and shot him. Ballistics are going to match your gun to the weapon that killed Strauss."

Owens smirked, "Good luck, 'cause the guy was sliced open—"

He snapped his jaw shut, eyes wide, staring at the two detectives in utter shock; he'd let his anger get the better of him. People could lie, but their emotions couldn't (at least, not most of the time). Slumping down into his seat, he scowled furiously at the table. How Strauss had been killed was left out of the media, giving them the perfect weapon to use to against idiots like Matthew Owens. They had him now.

"I want to make a deal," he muttered.

"D.A.'s not gonna make a deal with the guy who butchered a reverend," Hyde said. "You might as well give us a full confession."

"I was there, but I didn't kill him," he gripped his fingers together. "And you're wrong, Roan didn't send me. I saw him go into the alley, following some kid, I think, I couldn't tell. As soon as I walked by, I head something, I don't know what but I saw shadows moving in the alley. The priest, he had a gun, fired a few shots, but that didn't do anything whatever was trying to kill him. Next thing I know, blood's flying everywhere. Then there was that kid, just standing there."

"What kid?" Chavez asked anxiously, sliding a picture of Ozawa, taken yesterday, forward, "This one?"

"No," he said. "He was a little older, with tattoos, I think, and—"

He stopped midway, staring down at the table, body starting to shake, eyes bulging out of his head like he'd seen a ghost. Just as they were about to press him for answer, Owens started screaming his head off. He stood up again, clapping his hands over his ears, trying to block out some kind of offensive noise. He whipped his head from side to side, ignoring the protests of the detectives to sit down, the door flying open and two bodies tackling him to the ground. When they managed to free his hands from his head, all parties were stunned by the sight of blood spurting out of each ear. Owens strained his voice as he screamed, reaching octaves not possible for a man his age. After minutes of agonizing screaming—and just as the paramedics arrived—his head lulled to the side, eyes bugging out, mouth gaping in terror of some unseen force.

Owens was dead.

***

"How the hell did this happen?" Braddock boomed as he conducted his own interrogation on the two detectives. This time, he didn't give them the courtesy of chewing them out in his office. Instead, he did it for the entire squad to see; *they* had the decency to pretend they weren't listening. Chavez and Hyde forced themselves to watch Braddock's face as it went through the motions. Looking away would mean they had something to hide, or that they were children who couldn't handle a public scolding.

They were neither.

"Captain," Hyde risked interrupting his superior's rant. "We don't know what to tell you. He started screaming, then he just went limp."

"He looked like he was trying to block out a sound," Chavez chimed in. "God knows it's not the strangest case we've ever worked on."

"If things keep up like this," Braddock growled, "It just might be your last."

Now the entire squad threw away all pretense of polite courtesy and stared at their three comrades in silent shock. Though Chavez thought she saw some of their eyes twinkle with the flame of ambition that burned so brightly in her when she became a full-fledged officer of the law. She looked at her captain, not in fear, but in pity; he was the one who would suffer the most if they failed to get a solid lead on this case, *all* their cases. He was too old for this, and he knew it, but there wasn't much else in his life, it seemed. That was something she could relate to.

Dr. Grace Marshall pushed through the officers to the center to report the findings of her autopsy to Braddock. She'd heard what he had to say and glanced at Chavez and Hyde in slight worry, but composed herself as she stood before the wild bear of a police captain. She met his annoyed gaze with her clinical stare, daring him to talk down to her, or belittle her in any way. He seemed to settle down, allowing her to speak with him in private, urging the two partners to listen in.

"Mr. Owens, aside from a liver that grievously damaged from years of alcohol abuse, was in perfectly good condition for a man his age. That was, until I examined his brain and found a pile of mush instead. It looked as if someone detonated a bomb inside."

"Anything else?" asked the captain.

"I think I know appeared to have suffered a massive what might have triggered it." "The blow he received that broke his nose. It could have caused enough pressure for whatever-it-was to finish the job."

Hyde said, "The doctors examined him for a concussion before we brought him in, but he refused and further attention."

"How did it happen?" Braddock asked.

Chavez managed to keep herself from saying a thing, her memories of Zero breaking the guy's nose in the church's Fellowship Hall replaying over and over. Had he known about Owens's condition? Did she allow a murderer walk away—*again?* Part of her argued that she was being paranoid, but another part countered that she wouldn't forgive herself if she didn't look into it. Without another word, she left the squad, once again to the protests of her captain and partner.

Reaching the parking garage, she got in her car and drove out onto the New Orleans streets, decked out in Halloween decorations. Neon lights glowing orange and yellow and white, some patterned into pumpkins, candy corn, and ghosts. Fake cobwebs, witches, cauldrons, and the like passed her by as she headed for one place, where she knew Ozawa would be.

Celui Qui Réfléchit.

Despite the searing anger boiling in the pit of her stomach, she managed to obey traffic laws (if only barely) and reach the shop without incident. Parking in the same spot she'd been in last night, she slammed the door hard and stormed over the shop. Shoving the door out of her way, she entered the shop, full of customers ready to buy someone else's junk. She wasn't in much of a mood to wait and, despite feeling grateful to LeBlanc for what he'd done for her last night, she grabbed her badge as flashed for all to see. "Get out, now."

Like reluctant cattle, they herded out of the shop while Maurice LeBlanc looked at her dumbfounded, becoming fearful when he realized the mood she was in. His eyes darted away from hers, looking at something on the other side of the store before focusing them somewhere else. There, decked out in his more familiar attire—and looking right at home in it—stood Zero Ozawa.

She moved toward him, closing the distance between them in a matter of milliseconds.

"Talk," she barked.

"If you wanted to find me, you should have felt out for my presence," he answered calmly. "I could tell from the moment you left the station that you were pissed and it was all aimed at me. What did I do this time?"

"You may have killed a man. Matthew Owens, one of the guys who broke into the church, the one who interrogated Alexis, and the guy whose head you slammed into the ground."

"I assure you that if I wanted him dead, he'd be dead," he answered her glare with a steely gaze of his own. He was angry, about what Alexis had said, and was taking it out on her. That was fine, since Chavez was pissed that she was getting her ass chewed out by her captain because she didn't know anything about the world Zero inhabited. She wasn't about to back down because the kid finally decided to get serious. Poor LeBlanc looked like a frightened puppy, watching two bigger dogs size each other up for a fight.

"No more games," she declared. "No more riddles, no more *bullshit*. I want the truth and you're going to give it to me. Now."

"I have been telling you the truth, Detective," he bit back. "The only problem I keep running into is your stubborn, bullheaded, attitude. You can't trust anyone, can you?"

"Said the kid wearing the mask."

"You have no idea what you're getting yourself into, even though I've explained it to you. This isn't some game. Keep treating it like one and you'll end up dead!"

"I'm afraid of you," she narrowed her eyes at him.

Ozawa looked ready to say something, but thought better of it. "I didn't say you had to be. But you are afraid of something, aren't you? Afraid of putting your trust into someone you hardly know, because you've done it once before, haven't you?"

"Shut up," she warned.

"I'm not going to hurt you, Detective," he took a step back. "If anything, I want to be your friend. Michael chose you for a reason; he left himself vulnerable in order to prepare *you*. And I can't let his sacrifice be in vain."

"He left himself 'vulnerable?" she asked. "What the hell does that mean?"

"When you awaken someone's aura, it takes a considerable amount of energy from your own. At first, your own aura treats it how the human body treats foreign bacteria. The result being the recipient of the energy—in this case, *you*—going through the same motions you did. If I hadn't eased the process, you'd have been bed-ridden for weeks, or dead altogether."

Chavez let the meaning of his words sink in, her righteous fury dissipating.

"You he..." she felt her heart being gripped in the angry fist of guilt. "He's dead because of me."

"No, he's dead because of whatever's out there," Zero argued. "Right now, we need to find out just what we're dealing with. And there's one man who can help us with that."

"Who?"

"Alex Roan."

Chapter 20

Bête Noir once again hosted an obscene amount of customers as it had the night nearly three days ago. The neon lights danced across the room in rhythm with those on the dance floors, the bars filled to the max, and various suits dining in the middle. This was an entirely different world than the one outside, a place where people escaped the daily concerns of life and found happiness in bottles of wine and loveless liaisons. It reminded Renee of how she'd been after divorcing Ricardo Kaplan. But those were the least of her worries as she and Zero pushed through the crowds. People stopped to take notice of the latter's outfit, but chalked it up to a dedicated Halloween spirit. The horrific holiday was only a week away, and for the longest time for Renee, that meant she and her partner would have to deal with some of the more unusual cases to come across their desks.

It had normally kept her busy and out of the house, so she never bothered putting up decorations, as opposed the Massey household, which seemed to transform over into a haunted house that wowed the neighbors and spooked the children.

She wondered if Halloween held some kind of significance with the *Mononoke*; she'd ask Zero about it later, once this case was solved and the murderer caught. What better way to find a criminal than to ask the man who was currently the head criminal in all of New Orleans? Alex Roan had gained too much of a foothold on the city to not be unaware of who was responsible, even if he hadn't known about it until it was brought up by the police. At least, those were the masked boy's feelings on the matter.

On their way to the elevator, they were intercepted by the same stiff who had been prepared to fight Marcus O'Mara. His eyes narrowed into calculating slits as he observed the two of them. It seemed like things would be a repeat of last time.

"Can I help you?" he grunted.

"Yes," Zero smiled. "You can, kindly, get out of our way." In the next split-second, he grabbed the stiff's tie and yanked him forward, smashing his forehead against the stiff's. His head rebounded into the wall behind him, his large frame slumping into a heap on the floor. If anyone around them had taken notice, they decided it was in their best interest not to interfere. Shaking her head, Renee pressed the button to summon the elevator, the doors sliding open moments later. The raven-haired teen stepped in first, holding the door open for her; she hesitated, her mind flashing back to three nights ago.

She was looking up at Michael Strauss, his rune-covered Desert Eagle aimed squarely at the heart of the wasp-like creature before it morphed back into Alex Roan. A shudder traveled up and down her spine, the seed of uncertainty taking root. What would happen if Roan decided to attack them? Could Zero handle him on his own, so near his "power source", all the while having to worry about protecting her? Then her mind stopped working, processing the words she had just been thinking about.

'Protect?' she thought, nose wrinkling at the word.

She was a New Orleans Police Detective, she was supposed to stand on equal ground with her colleagues. Not let some kid fight her battles for her, not hide in the corner while some killer prepared for another slaughter. She'd worked hard, suffered physically and emotionally, and earned the respect of her peers accompanied by the rank bestowed upon her. Squaring her shoulders, standing a little taller, and letting anger meld with the professionalism of a cop, she stepped into the elevator and punched the button to take them to the next floor. Moments later, they doors opened, allowing them entrance into the hallway.

Nothing had changed, it seemed, for the moans of unidentified—but without a doubt important—people, muffled by the doors, were heard. All leading to the end of the hall, to the office of Alex Roan. The two of them strolled down the hallway with a purpose, doing their best to ignore the sounds heard (Renee made note of Zero's burning ears, but said nothing). Once they were at the door, Renee's hand unconsciously reached for her gun, while Zero grasped the hilt of the katana on his back. She glanced at him and he nodded, telling her to move in.

Grabbing the knob on the door, she twisted it—to her surprise, it was actually unlocked—and shoved it open. Hand now grasping her weapons, she did quick scan of the room, eyes landing on the purpose for their intrusion. Roan sat back in his chair, watching them both with a polite glare, hands intertwined as they rested on the knee crossed over his left leg.

"Detective Chavez," he smirked. "Come to face your fears. Or, are you and Mr. Ozawa here to partake in the benefits provided to my exclusive clientele? I'd be more than happy to set up a room for you."

"You're going to answer a few questions for us, Roan," she spat.

"Should I call my lawyer?"

"Only if you want the world to see you for what you *really* are."

"It's your word against mine," he replied nonchalantly. "You two are the ones who forced your way up here, if the footage from the security cameras is to be believed. You also assaulted one of my employees in the process. How could do that to Mr.... Oh, what was his name?"

"Your 'concern' is touching, Alex," Zero quipped. "I do believe we can reach an agreement. After all, we all want the same thing, don't we?"

"How do you figure that?"

"I know how much you Contractors hate sharing your space," he placed his left hand on his hip, extending the other in a friendly gesture. "Oh, sure, you made a deal with him as soon as you discovered who he was. But what's stopping him from turning on you? Especially once he learns the secret to your never-ending supply of energy. If he hasn't already?"

At the mention of his closely guarded secret, Roan's eyes narrowed dangerously; Renee could sense his aura—it was starting to become a natural feeling—flaring up, like an explosive about to blow. Beneath the visible parts of his skin, something stirred, like over-sized veins pulsing, promising to lash out and annihilate them both. Renee grasped her gun a little tighter and waited for Roan to make the first move.

Zero continued talking, "I mean, how long would it take for word to spread just how Alex Roan manages to keep replenishing his reserves without ever having to dip into his own power. How he can easily shift from *Mononoke* to human form and vice-versa. That might be enough to draw all the contractors in—and you know how greedy they can be. It wouldn't take long for the miracle to become just another treatment. But, hey, you could at least trademark it into something, right?"

"You drive a hard bargain, Mr. Ozawa," Roan smiled while gritting his teeth. "I should have killed you the first time we met. Next time, I'll be sure to finish you off, if you don't fail against our 'tourist' tonight."

"So that's why those men were sent to the church to kill me," he nodded to himself, though Renee caught a slight falsehood in his statement, like he was holding something back. "And why Michael was killed. This contractor must have made a deal with its host."

"Care to fill me in?" Renee asked, still glaring at Roan.

"It quite simple," Zero began to explain.

"Yes, I'm sure it is," Roan interjected. "Just as I'm sure you can continue on your way out. Have a nice night, Detective. Hunter."

***

Once they were out and safely away from *Bête Noir* (the stiff Zero knocked out was starting to come to, and the two of them agreed it was better to avoid a fight), the young man continued his explanation.

Apparently, Contractors can also absorb the auras of their kills, so long as the body's remains are fresh and free of any decay. Depending on the kill, the amount of energy they absorbed could easily substitute for a host. The reasons they don't do it frequently is because of... certain policies—he refused to elaborate further. But when they decided those policies didn't matter, they would normally target victims based on their level of spiritual aura.

And Hunters were very much a delicacy; especially those of the Ozawa lineage.

"So when the Contractor killed Strauss," Renee surmised as she turned on the corner. "It couldn't have absorbed his energy because... he already gave it to *me*." She swallowed hard, a pang in her heart when she realized just how significant the gesture was. Strauss hardly knew her, yet he had trusted her enough to risk his life and grant her this—whatever it was. There something both touching and frightening about it; a sense of pressure that left her uneasy. But she couldn't dwell on that know.

"In a nutshell," Zero confirmed. "Now we just need to find the Contractor's host, then we can end this."

"By 'ending' them?" she sneered, unable hide her disgust what he was implying.

"God, no!" he shook his head. "I 've never killed unless it was absolutely necessary. If this person can be reasoned with, there won't be any need for violence. Often, those who forms contracts with the *Mononoke* do it because of the emotional state they're in."

"Emotional state, huh?"

"Like rage, despair, etc. Usually caused by things like: Rejection, humiliation, the loss of a loved one. Nowadays, people are sensitive to just about anything."

"Wait," she glanced at him while keeping her attention on driving. "You said a 'the loss of a loved one.' Like if someone you love is murdered? Would this emotional state have to be recent?"

"No. The only time an aura can disappear is if it's absorbed by a contractor, or the person in question dies. If not, then their emotional energy can last for years to come, especially if it's something like despair or anger. To a Contractor, it'd be the equivalent to addict snorting the finest cocaine around. But as I said, the strength really depends on how long a person dwells on the source of the emotions."

"Like, say, your parents being killed by some punks?"

"Exactly."

Renee pressed the gas pedal a little harder, her destination clear; if she was right, then she might know who the Contractor's host is.

Chapter 21

The sun vanished behind the horizon, the darkness engulfing the city of New Orleans, neon lights picking up the slack. Chavez stopped the car at the corner just shy of the police station, far enough away for Zero to avoid being seen, but close enough for her to pick him up once she had what they needed. He disappeared into the alley as she drove towards the station, entering the parking garage. Killing the engine, she got out and headed for the elevator, her destination: the squad room. Pausing for a moment, she considered her options; Braddock was sure to be furious with her given that she walked out without a word to anyone.

And then there was Hyde, who was sure to be growing weary of her running off without explanation, leaving him to carry her workload and bear her burdens. Swallowing hard, she took a few calming breaths and stepped into the elevator. Pressing the button for her floor, she leaned against the wall as the doors slid shut. In no time at all, she was on her floor and in the squad room.

Searching the area, her eyes landed on Hyde working at his desk, his expression tight with concentration. Sighing, Chavez walked to her desk, sitting down across from him, "Hey."

He glanced up over the screen and acknowledged her with a nod, "Hey. Find whatever you were looking for?"

"Yeah, sort of," she smiled. "You ran interference with Braddock?"

He nodded, "You know I once went deer-hunting and ran into one of the biggest bears you'd ever seen. I nearly soiled myself, dropped my rifle, and just stood there frozen until my buddy, Carlos, managed to scare it off. That still doesn't compare to dealing with the captain when he's fuming like a chimney."

"Right," she offered an apologetic smile. "Jack, I'm sorry. I know you said you're used to this, but that doesn't mean I have to keep leaving you out of things like this. We're partners, we watch out for each other. It's not supposed to be one-sided like this."

"Don't worry about it," he grinned at her. "My old partner, back in Boston, used to be the same way. But I'm not some kid, I don't need to be coddled and protected. And my feelings aren't so sensitive either. Just know that I've got your back, Renee."

Smiling in earnest now, Chavez started searching through her own files, "I might have a lead on our serial killer. I went to see what Alex Roan knows about this; of course, he told me— without *actually* telling me—that the same person who killed those people in the theatre killed Strauss and sent Owens and his goons to the church after Ozawa."

"What's the connection between the pastor, Ozawa, and the other victims?"

"Nothing," she said. "They were targeted for different reasons, but I think I might know what our other victims had in common. At each crime scene, the number of bodies was three. What's that tell you?"

The light bulb went off in Hyde's head, "There's only *one* target; the rest are collateral damage. Kill enough people, and the police we'll search for a serial killer instead of a man with an axe to grind with one person. And the only victims we were able to ID at each scene were Nathan Vega and Bruce Raymond."

"It's more than that," she said. "Think about it. Monique Reynosa, why would you risk leaving a witness? The department store and theatre were both damaged by Katrina to the point that there was only one way in and out. You'd plant yourself in front of that exit to make sure no one got out of there alive. So why spare Monique?"

"She's involved," Hyde decided.

"Yes and no," Chavez replied. "Her motives the same, but might not have had anything to do with it. That doesn't mean she didn't know who was involved. That's why she was silenced later. That, and because of the symbolism."

"Symbolism?" Braddock asked from behind, startling them both. "Don't let me interrupt, you were on a roll. I want to hear this theory."

"Shouldn't we call O'Mara?" she asked.

"You snooze, you lose."

"Alright," she continued. "Both times, three people were killed, but Bruce Raymond was forced to watch his boys' slaughter. Basically, a 'look what's in store for you, pal.' What are the odds that the same thing happened to Nathan Vega? Get one last scare in before doing the deed?"

"It did," said the captain. "We wanted to keep that detail a secret just in case it was relevant; looks like it was."

Typing in the names of their only identified victims, Chavez watched the as the computer performed a search, running their names against the database. Seconds later, several cases popped up, but only one caught her attention; the one that proved her theory. It was a newspaper article that read in large letters:

COUPLE KILLED IN SENSELESS SHOOTING

Marco and Vickie Reynosa, 34 and 32 respectively, were enjoying a ride through the French Quarter when their car was fired on. Marco, who was driving, swerved into a ramp and the car flipped over, bursting into flames and trapping the couple inside. Thanks to the efforts of several good Samaritans, the couple's son, José, and daughter, Monique, were pulled to safety. Sadly, Marco and Vickie were killed in the resulting explosion, leaving their children orphaned. The only solace these young ones can take from this tragedy is the knowledge that their killers have been arrested. Nathan Vega, Bruce Raymond, and Mitchell Sanders, have all been arrested and are awaiting charges. When asked why they killed the couple, Vega replied, "We were just killing time until that new movie."

Chavez scrolled down to the next article:

KILLERS OF REYNOSA COUPLE RELEASED ON TECHNICALITY; PUBLIC OUTRAGED

Today, public outcry was at an all-time high when Nathan Vega, Bruce Raymond, and Mitchell Sanders were set free following a dismissal. The three teens, on trial for the murder of Marco and Vickie Reynosa several weeks prior, walked out of the courthouse today as free men, thanks to an error made by labs. Apparently, one of the workers filed the evidence improperly, forcing the judge to dismiss the case. The three teens were all smiles as they were escorted from the courthouse into the rabid crowd of protestors. There is no word on when the District Attorney will refile charges, nor have we managed to reach José and Monique Reynosa, the couple's children, to learn their reaction.

Chavez had read the articles out loud for Hyde and Braddock to hear, the trio sharing in their disgust of the situation. These three monsters had murdered two people and ruined two lives all for the sake of alleviating "boredom." It was sickening, that there were actually people willing to end lives for so little reason. And the fact they'd gotten away with it, because of a simple mistake by the lab, equally sickening. Chavez scrolled down to one final article:

MEMBER OF REYNOSA KILLER TRIO O.D.s

More than one year after being released on a technicality for the murder of Marco and Vickie Reynosa, Mitchell Sanders was found dead in what appeared to be an accidental overdose of heroin. Sanders, after being released, apparently severed ties with his accomplices, Nathan Vega and Bruce Raymond, and remained off the grid until today. There is some speculation that the overdose was intentional, that Sanders perhaps was haunted by his guilt over the murders of the Reynosa couple. Whatever the case, José and Monique Reynosa, who remain lost in the foster care system, can at least rest a little more comfortably knowing that one of their parents' killers is dead.

"So Sanders O.D.s," Hyde observed. "Lucky bastard."

"Means there's a gap in this little rampage for vengeance," Braddock crossed his arms. "What's that tell us?"

"That our killer is obsessed with killing three people," Chavez said. "That his way getting back at the remaining two while satisfying his desire to act out his fantasies of what he'd do to all three. The other two that were with them each time were just..."

"Collateral damage," Braddock and Hyde said at the same time.

"Which means we have two suspects," Chavez declared. "Monique Reynosa, who we know is no longer involved due to her death, but was left alive long enough for one reason. To make us think our only remaining suspect was among those killed."

She brought up a picture of a young boy, smiling in a photo taken before his world was shattered. A boy who was now a young man, consumed by avenging his parents' deaths that he apparently made a deal with a *Mononoke*. Once he'd tracked down the two men responsible, and made sure they suffered before dying, that's when things went south. He no longer wanted to be drained of his life energy by this monster, so they'd come up with a new deal: kill the two known Hunters in New Orleans and let the creature take their energy instead. Which involved luring Michael Strauss to a bar on Bourbon Street under the guise of a youth seeking guidance.

Taking advantage of Strauss's kindness, he fed the men to the beast, unaware that the energy that was to be absorbed had already been given to someone else. She could only imagine that this left the contractor angry and willing to suck the boy dry right then and there. But he'd convinced his parasite that he could kill the last Hunter: Zero Ozawa.

To that end, he decided that he couldn't risk the police identifying him, so he chose to eliminate the last remaining link. So, this young man killed his own sister by using her allergy to peanuts. Now, he was searching frantically for Ozawa while his parasite conducted its own search; probably planning on double-crossing him even if he managed to kill Ozawa.

Renee Chavez came to this conclusion as she stared at the photo of a young José Reynosa.

Chapter 22

Detectives Chavez and Hyde rode in silence down the street to José Reynosa's last known address, all the while being tailed by Zero Ozawa via the rooftops. After Braddock decided to check on her theory and looked up José—the kid had a record—he sent them on their way. He'd been arrested after assaulting a guy who threw a glass of beer in his face. It took three guys to separate them, the guy who threw the beer not getting charged due to familial connections. Probably did nothing to endear the poor kid towards the law after already having his parents denied the justice owed to them by the courts.

Chavez couldn't think of any reason for her partner not to come, especially given all he had to put up with the last three days, so she let him drive. She'd first spotted Zero on the rooftops after they were three blocks away from the station. The masked teen was a quick-learner, it seemed.

She pulled out her cell phone and dialed Marcus O'Mara's number, waiting for several rings before the voicemail answered. Leaving a message about their findings and where they would be, she hung up. She stared at her phone suspiciously for a few seconds; something wasn't right. There was a knot in her stomach, her body's way of telling her bad things were sure to happen.

"So why he'd choose those locations?" Hyde inquired. "What was the significance of the store and the theatre? The only thing they had in common was Katrina."

"Not the *only* thing," Chavez answered. "Marco Reynosa worked at the department store as a manager. Vickie was an aspiring theatre actress who'd just gotten her big break. She was going to star in the *Count of Monte Cristo*. And it was going to be at that exact theatre; it was also going to open on the day of Raymond's murder several years ago. That's why he waited a month after killing Vega."

"So there's an emotional connection?" Hyde concluded. "Does that mean he's likely to be hiding somewhere with the same significance? What about their old house?"

"Destroyed by the hurricane. Our best bet is if we search his house, then we'll learn something."

"I just don't get it," Hyde muttered. "His own sister. I get not wanting to be identified by the police, but why... why kill her? You'd think he want her to share in avenging their parents."

"Revenge can you make do things, Jackson," she offered. "Things you wouldn't do in a sound state of mind. Losing your parents, being bounced around foster care while their killers go free, and witnessing a side of the law that doesn't inspire any faith in the police. That can leave you in anything but a sound state. I almost feel bad for this kid; save for the fact that I think he killed Michael Strauss."

"What makes you think that?"

"The way our victims were killed suggested a sharp blade, right? And we already know José has no problem killing anyone to make it look random. I don't think the whole 'killing in threes' would apply to Strauss or Monique. Unless he's planning on a third victim." *Zero Ozawa.*

Hyde pressed the brake pedal gently and pulled to a stop, just outside of José's apartment.

***

Chavez and Hyde followed the land lord up the stairs to José apartment, the man muttering how the "brat hadn't paid his rent yet before dragging cops to his complex." He'd initially been reluctant to let them in without a warrant, until they "insisted" that keeping this quiet was the best thing for all involved (i.e. they promised to make sure any all future tenants knew that a dangerous criminal used to live here). And so, while muttering a few curses, he grabbed his large ring of keys and led the way up.

The apartment complex seemed a little too nice to place a man obsessed with revenge, as José supposedly was, to be living here. The walls were lined with pictures depicting the buildings long history, flower vases sitting atop tables in the hallway; lush green carpets mapping out the way to each room and painted a calming ocean blue. Then again, most serial killer turned out to be kind of person you'd least expect to have literal skeletons in their closet. It was all relative, in a way.

152

Stopping outside the room, they waited as the land lord knocked on the door, "Josie! Cops are here! Get the hell out!"

"Charming," Hyde whispered to Chavez, who nodded, amused. When there was no answer, the land lord searched the ring for the right key and unlocked the door. He stood aside as the two detectives entered the apartment, giving it a once over. There was barely any evidence that someone was living here; many of the boxes were still open; there was no television or computer; and there was a blow-up mattress that served as the bed. However, there was a plethora of books, each covering a different section of the supernatural.

I miss the days when kids stuck to using voodoo dolls, Chavez thought, frustrated. The notion was definitely more preferred to summoning demons and basically offering your soul to them. Especially if you're just going to chicken out in the end.

Instead of dwelling on the fact any further, she and Hyde pulled on their gloves and started searching. Nothing suggested he'd been here recently, but they were in luck; a phone had been set up and several messages were left behind. Hyde looked to his partner for confirmation (receiving a nod) and checked the messages.

"José, we need to talk," a voice, all too familiar to both detectives stated. *"Let's meet at the usual place."*

The land lord switched his focus between the two detectives, head tilted a slight fraction. He didn't know what the hell was going on, but from the looks on their faces, nothing good could come of it, especially if it damaged his apartment's reputation. He was about to see how he could negotiate with them to keep him out of the papers when Chavez threw one of the books she'd picked up across the space into the kitchen, cursing, "Son of a bitch!"

Hyde dialed the number of the station and spoke, "Get me through the Braddock... Sir, we may need to put out a BOLO for Marcus O'Mara."

Chavez pulled up a photo of O'Mara from a news article on her phone and held in front of the land lord for him to see. He squinted his eyes and leaned in to get a clear look at the photo before she yanked away and stuffed it in her pocket.

"Have you seen him before?" she asked none too kindly.

"Yeah," he said. "That's José's dad, isn't it?"

Chapter 23

Whenever Renee Chavez was pissed, she wouldn't be your first choice to ride in a car with; especially if she were at the wheel. Hyde knew better than to critique her driving at a moment like this, sucking up his complaints and glancing out the window. The streets flew by in a haze of colorful variants, the sounds of cars honking in the background. He braced himself when she turned onto the street and thanked God they were at the station. Anymore of that and he would've lost his lunch, not that he blamed Chavez for being so pissed off. Hell, he was pissed off too, he was just the type to keep locked up until the timing was right. And it would be right once he got his hands on that rat bastard Marcus O'Mara.

When they had recovered from the slight shock of learning that Marcus O'Mara was José Reynosa's father—*adopted* father, it seemed—they called it in. Braddock ordered them back to the station so they could coordinate, much to Chavez's chagrin. But she conceded that the last thing they needed was for her to run, head first, into a situation without all the facts. Just because O'Mara had been José's caregiver didn't mean he was helping him commit these murders. As much as people thought of him as a lone cowboy, those who knew him well enough had often said he had too much respect for the law to condone something like that.

It didn't change the fact that he knew how José must have felt about Nathan Vega and Bruce Raymond. If what Monique told Renee was to be believed, he'd been tossed around the foster care system, having nothing to hold on to except his desire for revenge. Much as Hyde hated to admit it, he couldn't blame the kid for what he'd done.

Back in Boston, the case had made the news there; Hyde and everyone he knew were disgusted with those three punks. He had to manage a riot that broke out when the judge dismissed the case. It always amazed him how a case like that can stir up such an uproar throughout the country. Part of him had been disappointed to learn that Mitchell Sanders died of a drug overdose. He would have loved to see that fear on his face moments before he would be forced to save him and stop José. He shook his head, clearing away those dark thoughts, wondering just how many more would make their way into his head the longer he was on the job.

Parking the car, Chavez and Hyde decided not to wait for the elevator and took the stairs, arriving in the squad room just as Braddock hailed them to his office. Duane Pierce was leaning against the window when they came in. Hyde resisted the urge to snap at the man, still very much discontented that he released Zero Ozawa. But now was not the time for petty grudges.

"Someone want to explain to me just what the hell is going on?" Braddock rumbled. "First we get called in on a massacre, the a priest gets butchered, followed by some crazy kid in a mask—who you let go by the way, Pierce—now it turns out that the lead detective on the case is related to our prime suspect? Did someone break a mirror, walk under a ladder, cross paths with a black cat, and manage to piss off a voodoo priest?"

"According to one my Assistant D.A.s, José Reynosa is one of O'Mara's informants from his days in Narcotics. He helped bring down some of major up-and-comers before they became credible threats."

"And O'Mara took the credit for each bust until he made Homicide, right?" Chavez scoffed. Her stomach boiled in anger; she hated men like O'Mara, who sat back and took all the credit while risking the lives of young kids. When she'd been in Narcotics, Chavez chose to do more undercover assignments rather than take that risk. In hindsight, maybe that was led to... She had to focus on the matter at hand, instead of letting past creep up on her. She continued, "At the apartment, the land lord swore that he was José's father."

"That's why I had my people find this," Pierce reached inside his jacket and produced a file. He handed it to Braddock, who studied it a moment, eyes widening a fraction before passing it on Hyde, who let Chavez look over his shoulder. They were official documents; proof of the adoption of José Reynosa by Marcus O'Mara. There was a collective sigh of frustration from the three officers. This was getting more and more complicated by the moment, and they still needed to find O'Mara and José before the contractor decided to check in on his host. As much as she was pissed at him, she wasn't about to let another murder happen if she could prevent. Though, it would validate her "killing in threes" theory that was made up to cover up the real reason for Michael Strauss's murder.

The detective in her would never let go of the fact that she lied on an official report, but the truth was far too bizarre for most of them to believe. Absentmindedly, she wondered just how many more of those kinds of cases she would have to cover up. As long as she was associated with Zero Ozawa, probably more than she would care to admit at the moment.

It got her thinking though, about something she would have to check on later when she was alone. She knew he was outside, waiting for her, but it would be difficult to ditch Hyde—she winced at the thought; he was her partner, after all. But putting an end to all this killing to precedence over her personal preferences.

"I'll talk to the neighborhood kids," she declared openly. "Odds are one of them knows José. If that's the case, maybe they know where he and O'Mara usually meet."

"They're not likely to trust a couple of cops," Hyde stated.

"Not if they don't think I'm a cop," she countered. "I just need to dirty myself up a little and pass myself off as anything but a cop. I'll ask around and call you with whatever I find."

"I don't like it," Braddock chimed in. "But we don't have the luxury of being picky at this moment. Go, make sure you're armed, and don't dig any deeper than you have to."

"Got it," she left the office and headed outside, where Zero Ozawa was sure to be waiting.

***

When she was far enough from the station, she ducked into one of the alleys and was met by Ozawa landing on his feet. Even in the darkness, she could tell he was (sort of) out of breath, leaning against the wall. He regarded her with an admonishing look, "I was barely able to keep up with you. What the hell did you find?"

"José Reynosa," she started. "When he was a kid, his parents were murdered by three street punks. Thanks to a mistake made by the labs, the guys walked. One of them died of an overdose, but we've identified the other two, both victims in the slaughters. That's why he struck a deal with this contractor, to make them pay, but he couldn't pay the price, so he decided to sell out Michael Strauss in exchange, but that didn't work out too well. That leaves you, the only person who can keep José from getting the life sucked out of him, literally."

"Well, don't I just feel all warm and fuzzy?" he deadpanned.

"Can you find Marcus O'Mara, the detective who was present when we interrogated you last night? As in sense his aura, or something?"

"That would be hard," he admitted. "At least, normally it would, but luckily for you, I was able to plant a tracker on him back at interrogation. You'll recall that he was the one who tackled me when I 'broadened your horizons.' That enabled me to get a feel for his aura; for all of yours. Even if a normal person's aura is weak, they're still unique to that person. I increased the potency of the trackers when I got a look at all of you during the interrogation, when you were all discussing what to do with me."

Zero followed her to the car and sat in the back, cross-legged, arms stretched out, middle and ring fingers curled. Taking in a deep breath, he let his mind wander, the spiritual network of auras flooding inside. Like a computer, he began to track the movements of Marcus O'Mara, searching the entire city for him. Given that he was just a normal man, it was going to be hard, but that was what the tracker was for. An old trick taught to him by his grandfather.

Channel a piece of your aura into a small orb and tag someone with, then increase the potency of its "signal" to be able to track it anywhere. It was how he knew Jackson Hyde was with Detective Chavez when he brought her home from the station. Now it was just a matter of locating the other detective.

It was simple enough, he could feel the small piece of his own energy all the way across town, in a place where most people wouldn't go. He closed in, the dark outline of the city speeding by, and found what he was looking for. It was an old house, heavily damaged by Hurricane Katrina, but still standing somehow. In the darkness of the mental image, he saw the light, blinking, giving off O'Mara's position. The tracker reacted to his emotional state, which was burning with frustration and anger. He could also feel a sense of conflict; a decision that he didn't want to make, but had to. O'Mara was going to arrest José for what he'd done, but not before the contractor killed them both.

When he opened his eyes, Zero noted the car was already in motion, Chavez glancing back at him through the mirror, waiting for instruction. Adjusting himself and strapping on the seat belt, he told her where to go, and sat back to think on how they would approach this. Odds were that this *Mononoke* was going to be ready for a fight, like it had been with Michael. Oh, the joy it must have felt when it realized he couldn't fight back, happily slaughtering him like lamb. He recalled the words of his father about forming attachments outside the clan:

"Those who exist outside our bloodline are just a means to an end. In war, the loyalties and comrades change, but the bonds of family will always remain strong."

He felt something in the back of his mind pulse painfully, as though it were disagreeing with that sentiment. Not that it would find much of a protest from him; he never saw anyone of his allies as "means to an end." They were no better or worse in his eyes, all equal partners. He felt Chavez pull the car onto the freeway and closed his eyes. When he opened them again, he saw they were in a small suburban neighborhood.

He told her where to turn and they were a block away from the house in no time at all, killing the engine and getting out. Crawling up to the house, they stopped just around the corner, watching the old structure under the ever-present gaze of the moon. The roof was caved in, a giant hold allowing light to shine in. All that remained of the windows were broken shards of glass still embedded in the seals. The front of the house was a gaping hole—the door that had likely been there once, was gone.

Chavez knew exactly what this place was; it was the house José and Monique had grown up in with their parents. The only thing he had other than his hatred, no matter how torn apart it was. For him, this was sanctuary, a place to think things over, and the home that had been ripped from him by those three men. But it was also his prison, the place tying him to his vendetta that he could never escape no matter how many holes there are. Kind of like her . . .

"Okay, I need to call this in," she dialed the station's number, about to press "Call" when Zero's hand stopped her.

"You can't seriously be thinking of bringing a bunch of cops here, while the *Mononoke* could be arriving any second."

"My guess is, it'll be too focused on you," she yanked her hand away. She called it in and hung up before Braddock could tell her to wait for back-up. She had enough with Zero beside her, besides, she wanted to beat the crap out of O'Mara first. "Now, all we have to do is—"

She was interrupted by Zero gently, but firmly, pressing his lips to hers, everything around her going blank for a few seconds. Afterwards, the hands cupping her cheeks let her go and he pulled his mask back into place. In the darkness she wasn't able to get a good look at his face. Despite the chilling wind, her face was hot, settling into an embarrassed scowl. Zero only grinned at her, "*Jii-chan* always said it was good luck to kiss a beautiful woman before running head first into danger."

"When this is over," she growled. "I am going to kick your ass."

"I look forward it, honey," he winked, leaving her where she was and walking toward the house. Taking a few deep breaths, she managed to rid her face of that annoying blush and followed. At the very least, she would have O'Mara to warm up on if things went south—which, in her experience, they normally did. She removed her gun from its holster and followed suit and stayed low, using the shadows to her advantage. Hugging the sides of the house not in ruins, she met Zero and gaping entrance, signaling him to wait while she checked things out.

Going in first, she grabbed a flash light; its beam cut through the darkness, giving her a clear look at what likely once a beautiful home, the smell of mold, the sound of glass being crushed beneath her shoes, and the faded paint on the walls that was likely washed away by the flooding. Furniture, water-damaged and frail, sat in the living room, an old television staring back at them with a cracked screen. A broken shelf stood next to an old door, which most likely led into the kitchen. Taking one side, she watched Zero, his hand readily grasping the katana on his back, before opening the door. Moonlight seeped through the massive hole in the ceiling, the entire kitchen basking in its eerie glow.

An old refrigerator lay on its front, revealing a nest of roaches when she shined her lights over there (Great, she thought with disgust, more bugs). Cabinets were opened, all content spilled out to the floor in the form of shattered, moldy, glass. A table sat in pieces on the floor in the middle, four chairs waiting to be filled. She could almost imagine what this place must have looked like in the years before Katrina. She could almost see the happy family getting ready for an ill-fated car ride into the city.

Behind her Zero could sense the presence of the *Mononoke,* this is where it had been summoned. He smiled bitterly and the cold irony; contractors preferred to suck the energy out of their hosts at the place of their summoning. When he hadn't cared what would become of him, José must have chosen this spot as his final resting place. It was almost poetic, in a chillingly frightening sort of way, but he focused on the task at hand. Stepping on more broken glass, he pressed down on something.

Stepping back, he crouched down and picked up what appeared to be a photograph; taking a closer look at the family pictured. He didn't think people still did family photographs anymore—it just seemed too old fashioned for kids of this generation. The smiling faces betrayed the tragedy that befell this family, innocent grins of the two children oblivious to lives they would lead later in life.

But he couldn't dwell on that now, given the presence he sensed behind him. He could feel them inch closer and closer, thinking they'd gotten the upper hand. When they were in reach, he spun on his heel and knocked the gun out their hand. They tried to punch him, wound up hitting the photo instead, glass digging into their skin. The yelp of pain that echoed through the darkness was enough for him to identify his attacker as male.

He kicked his lower leg, forcing to bend and bring to ground, broken glass shards biting at his knee. Quickly circling him, Zero brought his kunai to the throat of Marcus O'Mara.

Chapter 24

When Renee heard the struggle behind her, she pivoted on her heel and aimed her weapon at the two struggling shapes. Unable to get a proper aim without the risk of hitting Zero, she waited and decided to let the stronger of the two prevail. Despite his size and build, Ozawa managed to bring down his opponent and brought his knife to O'Mara's throat, the cold steel pressing against a vein in his neck. He kept his free hand on the back of the detective's making sure he couldn't do anything but look at her. She kept her gun trained solely on O'Mara's figure, glaring coldly at the man. He answered her with a stern defiance in his eyes, somehow able to look down on her from his position.

"You've got a lot of explaining to do, Marcus," her tone was clinical, ready to shoot him if he managed to get free of his captor.

"Looks like I'm not the only one," he spat, glancing his eyes up at Zero. "You got a thing for younger guys, Chavez? Or just suspects who managed to overpower you? I'm not here to judge, just wondering if this is an ideal first date."

"José," she got to point rather than entertain O'Mara's jab. It was true, though, she'd have to explain to both Hyde and Captain Braddock why Ozawa was here, but that was best confronted later. Studying him, she caught the tension in O'Mara's body at the mention of his adopted son. "I'm guessing who you know it's against policy to involve yourself in cases where you're related to the prime suspect. But you still took lead on this case, anyway, hoping to get him off for this."

"You're wrong!" he struggled against the masked boy's grip. "I was going to bring José in. I just wanted to make sure he wasn't in a body bag when it happened! That some ambitious officer didn't shoot him and use it to further their career. I was trying to keep this from becoming some big scandal."

"Oh, it's a scandal alright," she mocked. "'Local Detective Related To Serial Killer, Tries To Cover It Up.' That'll make it all better."

"You don't get it," he shook his head. "José didn't do this. He couldn't have done this. Yes, he hated Vega and Raymond for what they did, but we both agreed it was better for them to rot in prison cells instead of killing them out right. That even though it would take a while, we could bring them down. The bigger they got, the more satisfying it would be when they finally fell."

"And the faster you'd climb the ladder, right?"

"This was never about me! It was about giving him closure, giving his parents the justice they should have gotten years ago. It was an open-and-shut case, but they walked because the lab screw up! What the hell kind of justice is that? I almost turned in my badge when I found out."

"You should have," Renee said. "Would have saved us a lot of trouble."

"I think we need to hurry this up," Zero interjected, sparing a glance at Renee before focusing on O'Mara again. The single second was all she needed to know what was happening; the *Mononoke* was on its way and getting closer by the second. They had O'Mara, but they still needed to get José somewhere safe. First, they had to find him.

"How'd you even find this place?" O'Mara asked. "No one, not even the press knew about the house. I kept it that way so José and I could have a place to talk, a reminder of why he was doing this."

"You shouldn't have kept him living in the past," she snapped. "Instead of helping him get through it, you only nurtured his hatred!"

"What was I supposed to do?!" he roared, once again struggling against Ozawa's hold, the kunai digging into his flesh, threatening to pop the vein that was throbbing angrily in his neck. "Just tell him to forget about, that he should just let go of what they did to his family? Is that what you would have done? Told him to forget what happened? Pretend that everything was normal?"

"You should have gotten him help! Taken him to a specialist who could have helped him come to terms with it.

Instead, you turned him into a C.I. Made him your rat in the drug ring, risked his life so you could make detective!"

"You think I *wanted* that to happen!" he managed to get to his feet before Zero forced him back down. His eyes were wide, teeth bared like an animal, face turning red from rage. "He volunteered! Said he wanted to help bring down Vega and Raymond. That if I didn't let him, he'd go another cop, one who might have gotten him killed! I couldn't stop him, but I could at least contain him."

"By dangling those two like steaks over a pit," she accused icily.

"He needed to build a reputation," he sighed, anger leaving him, visibly deflating. "We had to make it look like he was a dependable source. That meant he had to get that tats, spend a year in prison, turn himself into one of 'them.' It was the only to be sure he'd get there trust. I didn't want to use a C.I. Hell, no one does, but that's the only way to get the upper hand in this war."

"He didn't need a handler," she kept her tone even. "He needed someone to act as his father, to teach him the things Marco Reynosa would never be able to. Instead, you made him into what he is. He got impatient, decided to take matters into his own hands. Because of that—because of *you*—four innocent people are dead."

O'Mara choked out a humorless laugh, "I'd hardly call them innocent. Sooner or later, they'd be trading drug houses for holding cells and vice versa." He dropped his gaze to the floor, looking at the old family photo of José with his loved ones. He closed in eyes in what appeared to be shame, head bowing, whispering a prayer, perhaps asking Marco and Vickie for forgiveness. Renee snorted in disgust and looked up at Zero, who watched the man with slight compassion, but kept his hold firm. She reached for her cell phone, ready to call it in—

Bang!!!

The unmistakable report of a gunshot echoed through the abandoned house, Renee bringing up her weapon in response. Her eyes roamed over the old structure, trying to determine where the shot had come from. Heart racing, pulse pounding heavily in her veins, finger ready to squeeze the trigger at a moment's notice. Renee's scan settled on Zero, his own eyes wide, posture stiff, hold on O'Mara loosening. He stared right at her, their eyes searching one another for something, before collapsing to the ground.

"Zero!" she cried. *What the hell, shouldn't his body armor have protected him?*

She was about to run over to him, when she realized there was someone standing in the doorway. The shadow was shaking, unable to believe what it had just done, taking small, uncertain steps forward. When the figure finally stepped into the light, Renee Chavez found herself staring at José Reynosa.

***

"Drop your weapon!" she ordered, eyes constantly switching between him and the prone Zero Ozawa. After several seconds (minutes, they felt like minutes), he still hadn't moved from where he'd fallen. Renee saw blood pouring down his side, the small puddle resembling a black snake as it slithered into the moonlight, its bright crimson color standing out against the floor. O'Mara put as much distance between himself and Zero as possible, regaining his weapon in the process. Much to her surprise, he too was aiming for José.

"Do as she says, José!" he shouted. "I can't protect you if you don't cooperate!"

"I..." he breathed out, eyes never leaving the prone body on the floor. Chavez took in his appearance; he was thin, thinner than a boy his age should be. His shirt hung loosely around his arms and torso, cheekbones hollow, and eye-sockets more profound. In short, José's body showed signs of malnutrition, something that shouldn't have been possible. As much as she couldn't stand the sight to be in his presence at the moment, Chavez knew O'Mara cared for this boy too much. And it got her thinking: *Was this the price you paid when you make a deal with these monsters?*

José found his voice, "I d-didn't have a c-choice. I knew what would happen—it *told* me, but... I couldn't take it anymore! They had to pay!"

"They would have," O'Mara lowered his gun, eyes flickering towards Chavez, unsure of what she would do. "I made you a promise, didn't I? We'd bring them down the right way, let them rot in cages for the rest of their lives."

"You don't get it!" he yelled. "Even if they were in prison, they'd still have power, have influence over the world outside. They had to die, it was the only way for it all to end!"

166

"José," Chavez decided it was better for this to end without any more violence; besides, she knew from Zero's warning that the contractor was on its way. For all she knew, it was here already, watching from the shadows, and waiting for a chance to kill them all. "Just put the gun down and let us help you. I know you didn't want any of this, that you were forced to—"

"I *did* want this!" he bellowed. "I wanted them to die, to suffer, to watch and see what was in store for them, to see my face and know who I was before they died. God forgive me, I'm not sorry! I'm glad they're both dead!"

"And what about the other four people who died?" O'Mara whispered. "Why'd you kill them? A jury would've understood you killing Vega and Raymond, but there's no excuse for taking lives that had nothing to do with it."

Chavez decided to ignore the irony of the statement, given what he'd said only minutes ago. Her attention returned to Zero's immobile form, risking a move closer to him. José Reynosa noticed this and turned his weapon on her, shouting at her not to move. It was then, that she noticed he was carrying the Desert Eagle she'd seen Michael Strauss use against Alex Roan three nights ago. She met his aim with her own, ready to shoot him if necessary.

"S-stay away from him!" he stammered. "He's not making it out of this one."

"José, I can't let that happen. If he dies, that's just one more murder charge to the eight you've already racked up so far."

"You said you *knew*," he swallowed hard. "Then you know why he has to die. That's the only way it'll leave me alone. It was only supposed to be the priest, but—"

"José!" O'Mara snapped. "Not another word."

"It doesn't matter what he says or doesn't say, O'Mara," Chavez slowly took a step forward. "He's already confessed to murdering six people, one more won't make a difference. Besides, being in possession of that gun is proof enough that he killed Michael Strauss. Or at least, that he was an accessory. Isn't that right, José?"

The young man didn't seem to hear her, too busy searching for any sign that the contractor was on here. The thought sent a chill up and down her spine, tempting her to remain on look out as well. But she didn't trust O'Mara, had no way of knowing whether or not he'd shoot her to cover this whole thing up. Paranoid, she would admit, but it wasn't exactly unwarranted given his actions. A low groan from Zero drew all of their attention, the masked teen struggling to get to his feet.

"Damn it!" José cursed. "Just die already!"

"Don't even think about it!" she fired off a warning shot just passed him. He paused, giving O'Mara just enough time to tackle him to ground, the large gun sliding across the floor. While they struggled, she moved to the masked teen's side, examining the wound in his back. It was too dark for her to tell, and for a terrible moment, she wondered if the bullet had hit his spine. But when he managed to curl into a fetal position, the fear left her body.

Draping his arm around her shoulder, she helped him to his feet and went out the back door. He rested against the door, legs outstretched, breaths short and haggard. His face was tightened into a pained expression, but he managed to open his blue eyes and look at her.

"Some 'first date', huh?" he wheezed out.

"Don't you die on me, you little brat," she ground out through her teeth. "I still have to kick your ass when this is over."

"Unfortunately," he growled in pain. "We have more . . . pressing matters at the moment."

Before she could get him to elaborate, a loud crash startled her and she turned just in time to see O'Mara fly past her, body rolling across the grass before stopping just short of a tree. From this distance, she wasn't able to tell if he was dead of just unconscious; but that wasn't her most troubling concern at the moment. A bone-chilling scream erupted from the house, high-pitched and terrified. Ignoring her brain's desire to stay hidden—coupled with Ozawa's protests—Chavez grabbed her weapon and ran inside.

In the middle of the broken down kitchen, beneath the hole in the ceiling, José Reynosa was suspended in the air, bathed in the glow of the moonlight. His eyes were bulging out of their sockets, seemingly ready to pop out at any moment; his mouth was agape, sound no longer emanating from it. She wasn't sure if it was a trick of the light, or because of what the masked boy just outside the room had done to her, but Chavez watched as strings of light flowed out of José's body. His life energy, she realized with mixture of wonder and awe and dread; the more energy that was drained, the more his body deflated like a balloon. If he'd been struggling before, he'd stopped either due to loss of energy, or because he resigned himself to the fate promised to him by this monster.

She wanted to look away, but she couldn't, some disturbed part of her fascinated by what she was seeing. Besides, what good would her being able to move do, anyway? Regular guns were useless against the *Mononoke* if her encounter with Alex Roan was to be any indication.

Wait, she thought with a slight start, *regular* guns were useless; Michael Strauss's rune-covered Desert Eagle on the other hand . . .

José's body, drained of all life energy, was tossed aside like a crab shell after all the meat had been sucked out. That horror-filled expression was forever etched on to his face, his body twisted into an unnatural position. Just short of the pillar of light, a large shape shuddered in the darkness, relishing in its meal, savoring the taste.

Chavez never took her eyes off the creature, watching its every move, too afraid of what might happen should she take her eyes off it for more than a few seconds. It took a step forward, the pale moonlight washing away its shadowy cloak. Its true form was finally revealed; its upper body a large, black, mantis-like monster, hunched down as if praying, sharp pincers scraping against one another. The lower half of its body was a muscular pair of legs, two sharp talons protruding from each of its feet. Two large wings sprouted from its back, buzzing every minute or so in rapid movement.

It eyes, glowing an eerie red, followed her every move, pupils the size of a speck of dirt mimicking its subtle change in her stance. From its jaw, four mandibles flexed about, a drool falling to the floor, melting through the tiles. After sizing up its opponent for a few moments, it growled, "We finally meet."

She recognized the gurgling tone in its voice, like it was drowning; it had been there, speaking with Alex Roan, had been the one to obliterate that punk with the shuriken in his eye. The orchestrator of Michael Strauss's death, the one who'd forced José to kill his own sister, and the one who sent those goons, led by Matthew Owens, to the church to kill Zero. She swallowed nervously, her weapon trained on its torso, the exposed heart beating steadily.

"I see now," it continued, watching her carefully, "why the priest had no aura to offer me. How pathetic. By passing on his aura to you, he also ensured that yours will be a far worse death than his."

Chavez sucked in a breath, unable to fathom she was actually having a conversation (one-sided though it may be) with this monster. This *murderer*, who slaughtered people like they were cattle, was after the aura awakened in her by Michael Strauss, as well as the aura of Zero Ozawa, currently seated outside, no more than a few feet away. But there was one thing she wanted to know, a question that passed through her lips before she could stop it:

"Why?" she asked.

"Why?" it repeated, tilting its head in an inquiring manner, much like the young man in the theatre, just like Michael Strauss when she found him in kitchen of that bar on Bourbon Street. Was that its way of marking its victims, arranging their bodies in positions such as that? Or maybe it had read her mind, like Roan had, and was using it as means of intimidating her. If so, it was working, but she couldn't let it know that. The contractor chuckled, "For status of course. When word reaches that I managed to fell two Hunters, especially if one of them was the last of the Ozawa clan, *he* will reward me with a source of limitless energy. Something far less... 'restricting' as Roan's little orgies."

"Who are you talking about?" she pressed, trying to get answers. If Zero was listening in from the outside, the least she could do provide him with information of who was responsible for all this. This contractor was nothing more than another rung on a ladder. Where that ladder led to was likely something she wouldn't be able to figure out on her own. She needed to keep stalling for time, waiting for back-up to show up.

Not that it would make much difference against this beast of another world, but it was better to try something than to do nothing at all.

"I'm afraid that would be telling," he laughed. "And I more in the mood for a second course!"

It lunged at her, mandibles stretching to their limit, teeth ready to sink in to her flesh, and devour her whole. Willing her body to move, she dodged its advance, rolling out of the way, down on one knee, face scrunched up as she squeezed the trigger. Three shots to exposed heart, each bullet bouncing off with a *ding!*, much like that they had the last time she tried it. It did little more than annoy the contractor, who roared as it made a second attempt at her. This time, it swiped its pincer arms wildly, knocking her into an old cabinet.

Landing on the ground in a crumpled heap, she forced her eyes open and searched the floor, seeing a flash of silver. The Desert Eagle, Strauss's weapon, the only thing short of Ozawa's weaponry that could hurt the *Mononoke*. She had thought about grabbing one of Zero's weapons earlier, but in his current state, she couldn't take the risk that it would tip off the contractor to his whereabouts. But the bullets in that gun might be the only thing that would ensure she'd survived this night. She felt the presence of the creature loom over her, she had to think fast.

As it slowly descended toward her, she turned on her back and shot it point blank in the left eye. It recoiled, rubbing its eye like a bullet was nothing more than a speck of dust, but it provided enough of an opportunity for her to scramble across the floor, shards of glass digging into her palms. The contractor's pincer's followed her just short of her boots, cutting through the fabric of her right pant leg. Pain shot up through her leg and onward, but she pressed forward, only inches away from, perhaps, her only salvation. The contractor brought down another pincer, like a medieval guillotine, this time slicing through her shirt and into the flesh of her torso.

Gritting her teeth, another wave of pain washing over her, this time a little more severe, and deeper, Chavez through herself forward and touched the barrel of the gun. Scrambling into a sitting position against the wall, the detective managed to fumble with the gun and aim it at the creature. She could feel the blood running down her side, pain biting at her while the adrenaline kept it at bay. It was exactly like it had been that night in *Bête Noir* with Alex Roan and his true self. The contractor slowly advancing on her, her back against a wall—or elevator as the case had been then—her will refusing to allow her to give in to the fear that consumed her.

Chavez sucked in a few breaths to steady her speeding heart and aimed squarely for the exposed heart. Though it conveyed no visible signs of distress, the contractor's organ began beating slightly faster, as if it knew what was in store for it. Making sure it was loaded, she squeezed the trigger three times, each shot flying toward the monster. The recoil pushed her further against the wall, arms dropping to the floor. After the loud *boom!*, she forced herself to look up, at her handy work.

Nothing happened; nothing at all.

The contractor was still standing there, pausing only out of shock that it had not been destroyed by the gun. It glanced down at the ground, the gnarled and dented bullets lying beneath it as if they were nothing. Nothing but more rubble on the floor of the destroyed home. For a moment, time stood still, neither of them moving, and their attention focused solely on the spent rounds. Then, both lifted their gazes from the floor and looked each other square in the eye.

The monster's face split into a large grin, teeth bared once more, drool pouring from its mandibles, and continued its slow advance. The predator had secured its position of superiority over the meaningless prey, who thought it could actually defy the natural order. The pinchers scraped across the floors, cutting through the tiles, eliciting a scratching sound that was sure to frighten anyone else.

But all she could do was replay everything she had done and compare it to what she'd seen Strauss do that night. Where had she gone wrong? What had different this time, save for the obvious? Risking a glance away from her attacker, she studied the runes that ran along the barrel of the gun, and realized something she hadn't noticed that night. Rather, she hadn't been able to see it due to her lack of knowledge of this unusual world.

Strauss had channeled his aura into the weapon and around the bullets; that was how he was able to hurt the *Mononoke*. That was why he had failed to kill the contractor when it attacked him in the alley that night. It was something she wasn't able to do yet; or at all as the case seemed.

Leaning her head back against the wall, she thought of her ex-husband, Ricardo; Mary Beckett, her former best friend; her partner Jackson Hyde. Many others appeared, from her parents to her coworkers at the precinct. And, dammit all, she felt her eyes start to burn with unshed tears, her pride refusing to let her cry and give this monster the satisfaction. Once again, she resign herself to her fate, part of her—larger than she would admit—hoped that some kind of miracle would happen to her again. That someone would stop this thing before she became its next meal.

But she knew that it was nothing more than wishful thinking, a pitiful desire to stay alive. It was then, that she finally registered the contractor's proximity to her, mandibles reaching out, scratching at her face. She wasn't how, but she could feel the energy start to leave her, a sort of burning that prompted her to cry out in pain. Eyes tightly closed, she did her best to fight back any way she could, but it was worthless. Chavez could easily picture the grin on the face of this monster.

Then it happened.

Chapter 25

Renee had once again readied herself for death, for the realization that she'd never fully understand the world behind their own. She was ready to die, much as she wanted to deny it; the job never guaranteed survival. Whether it was drug dealers, serial killers, or just some punk with a gun and chip on the shoulder, Renee Chavez never deluded herself into thinking she wouldn't be killed in the line of duty. It was a hazardous work environment, and she wouldn't have traded it for anything else in the world. Not even a stable marriage, a part of her mind jeered, but she ignored the self-jab.

She had been ready for the horrific fate that awaited her, had felt whatever energy awakened in her start to be drained rather painfully. Then, it stopped, and there was nothing but the world around her, closed off by her own eyes. She didn't know what that meant, however, and wondered for one, dreadfully hopeful moment, that she was still alive, that something had happened. But that was false hope; it had to be, otherwise she might actually start thinking of a retirement plan when the time came. Deciding there was only one way to know for sure, Renee opened her eyes, pupils readjusting to the light.

That's when she saw him standing in front of her— between her and the contractor—the wound from earlier still noticeable, but of seemingly little importance. In his hands, he wielded his katana, ready to cut through the furious monster before him. Hunching low, he took a stance and readied for battle.

"Going to sit there all day, Detective?" Zero Ozawa inquired while never taking his eyes off his opponent. He didn't look at her, but she could picture his masked face, eyes narrowed, jaw set, doing his best to ignore the sharp pain from the gunshot wound. But there was something different; his voice, it sounded deeper for some reason. When he turned his head to look at her, she was struck by the sight of his eyes.

They were no longer blue like the ocean, but different color; a steely silver.

Gone was any of the warmth he'd shown her earlier, instead watching her with an emotion she suspected was disinterested annoyance. He clicked his tongue at her and turned back to his opponent, "Idiot, making me do all the work while you sit on your ass."

That was enough for to forget her aching leg and side, anger burning in her gut again. Grinding her teeth together, she countered his insult, "You're one to talk, you little—"

"Who said I was talking to *you?*" he snapped. She stared at him, dumbfounded for a moment while he continued: "Just pick yourself up and get out of the way. Better yet, sit there while I let our friend here finish what he started on you. That way I can get a clean kill and get some use out of you if all you're going to do is whine."

Despite the dire situation she found herself in, Renee found glaring furiously at the masked boy's back. What the hell was wrong with him? He was acting like a completely different person than the eccentric teen who'd stolen a kiss from her. She stopped thinking about that, not in the mood to relive the embarrassment, and focused on what was happening right now. The contractor decided they'd done enough talking and lunged forward.

"Die, Ozawa!" it screamed.

Taking its pincer-arms, it swung them forward in rapid succession, intent on ripping them both limb from limb. Instead, he only crashed through the wall to the backyard, shaking off the rubble with annoyance. Before it could recover, a shadow shot out from the house and dragged its katana across the lower half of the torso. Pain shot through its body and it curled into itself with a howl of pain. Just before Zero could strike again, the contractor side-stepped him and rammed its body into his, sending him back into the house.

Resting on the floor, he lifted his head to meet the hollowed out gaze of José Reynosa, the boy who shot him. Making a "tch" sound, he resumed a vertical base, glancing at Detective Chavez, safety tucked away in the corner. She continued watching him in both awe and suspicion; clearly she was unnerved by him. Behind his mask, he was free to smirk and looked back towards his main concern. Deciding there had been enough playing around, he held *Araguru-getsu-ga* under the gaze of the moon, allowing the blade to absorb the ethereal light.

Projecting his own energy in through the hilt, the katana glowed with a magnificent light, illuminating the rest of the room. Renee watched with fascinated interest as the apparent "last of the Ozawa" crouched down, twisting slightly, and waited. The contractor roared violently as it charged, arms outstretched, appearing as if he was trying to engulf him. As it reached the doorway, Zero swung forward. The burst of energy blinded the nearby detective, who had to close her eyes.

The contractor's horror-filled scream echoed into nothingness as the light died down.

When she opened her eyes, the only evidence of the creature's existence was a pile of ash that formed a trail leading outside the house. Whatever Zero did completely destroyed the *Mononoke* and put an end to all this. He took deep breaths, chest heaving, and looked at her, sizing her up. Looking back to the outside, he gestured to the prone form of Marcus O'Mara, who'd completely missed the entire exchange. Only now was he regaining consciousness, struggling to get to his feet.

Renee stood up, her leg screaming in pain now that the adrenaline had left her, and limped outside, hand still on her torso where she'd been cut. Zero followed, making sure she didn't step over the ash. When she was close enough, she nearly collapsed, only to be caught by the young man behind her, who sneered at her with annoyance. She ignored the change in his personality and focused on O'Mara, who was groaning in delirium. When he turned on his back, he looked up at her, "J-José . . ."

Renee bit her lip, not sure of what she should tell him, or if she should even allow him to see what remained of his adopted son. Though she held nothing but contempt for the man, it didn't make telling him this terrible news any easier. But when he saw the look in her eyes, all she had to do was shake heard in the negative to convey the news. He let his head fall to the grass and blinked his eyes rapidly, trying to keep the tears from falling. Renee glanced at Zero, his back to her, hunching over the pile of ash; he wasn't going to be of any help.

However, she realized he was doing something, a small flicker of light illuminating his skull-masked face in the darkness. When he stood to his full height, she saw the fire that quickly travelled along the trail of ash towards the house. For a moment, she didn't know what to do, the rational part of her mind trying to fathom that he'd just set *ash* on fire. When the flames crawled inside, an explosion of fire erupted from the house, the force pushing her to grass. Zero helped her up, explaining to her, "It's better if they don't know what happened here. That they think he killed himself rather than wonder what happened to the body."

Even though she didn't agree with it on a professional level, her inner morality told her it was the right thing to do. O'Mara rose to a kneeling position, sitting on his knees while he stared at the house. The house once shared by a happy family four, now a fiery grave for one tortured soul. Trying to stand on her own, she hissed as gash in her leg started to ache, an event that didn't go unnoticed by Zero Ozawa. He gave a small sigh of annoyance while setting on the grass gently, looking her in the eye.

"It'd be much easier if you stopped moving," he suggested. "You're already losing a lot of blood. Keep moving around and you'll lose even more. I think it's best if you get some much-needed rest, Detective."

Before she could reply—or protest—his silver eyes began to glow, much like they had done in the precinct (when they'd been blue). The effect was the same as well; her vision blurred until it all went black, the sound of sirens not far off in the distance.
***

Renee hadn't realized it at the time, but this feeling of time slowing down was something she would have to grow accustomed to. The feeling that the entire world had melted away, leaving only this moment, with these select group of people. In this case, they were herself, her husband Ricardo, and best friend and Maid of Honor at the former two's wedding, Mary Beckett. Renee immediately pieced things together by what she was seeing (although you didn't need to be a cop to know what was going on); the bottle of wine, the two half-naked people in front of her, and their expression was the evidence she needed to confirm everything. They were having an affair, her mind registered after it ceased working for a few moments.

While she'd been hanging from a ceiling, repeatedly getting punched and having her ribs bruised or broken—she couldn't remember which right now—they'd been having sex in the bed where she and Ricardo had spent so many sleepless nights. Where they had marked the first night of their marriage after coming home for the first time as husband and wife. Where she had, admittedly, been absent for the last few months.

While she was lying in the hospital, fearing whatever reprisal Alex Roan had in store for her, and where Ricardo fit into it, they'd been enjoying the pleasures of each other's flesh. Now, where her mind had once been captivated by fear of what Roan would do in retaliation to her infiltrating his gang, a dark part of her, newly born and emerging quickly, hoped it involved something horrific befalling both Ricardo and Mary. Oddly enough, even though she was practically boiling with rage on the inside, she was fairly certain none of that anger was making it outward.

Her introspection was interrupted by Ricardo's voice, "Renee, what the hell happened to you?"

There was something in his voice; not guilt, or fright, it was concern.

Concern, her mind repeated to itself, the bastard actually had the nerve to show concern for her physical well-being right now? All while standing in his underwear, caught red-handed in an affair with his wife's Maid of Honor? The anger, the hurt, and all the other emotions swirling inside her began increasing speed, a hurricane threatening to break free the longer she stayed there. So, she decided it would be best for all parties if she just left, suddenly too tired to deal with this after the night she'd had.

Without another word, she turned her back to them and started toward the cab that was still parked outside the house. Unfortunately, neither of them was willing to just let her go without some sort of explanation. Mary Beckett pushed past Ricardo, stepping on to the cold grass with nothing protecting her feet.

"Renee!" she grabbed the officer's shoulder. "Wait, what happened—?"

The instant she felt Mary's touch on her shoulder, the anger inside of Renee burst through the dam of control she'd constructed. Body tensing, she spun on her heel and, right hand clenched into a fist, and smashed it against Mary's nose. With a shriek of terror, she was sent to the ground, nose broken, blood on her face and staining Ricardo's shirt. Renee loomed over her, breathing heavily, her good eye burning with tears of rage and despair at their nonchalance at what was a clear betrayal. In an instant, Ricardo was at Mary's side, examining the damage done.

"Renee . . ." he tried, moving toward her.

"Don't," she growled, hand still clenched, ready to strike him if he should enter her personal space.

"Please, let me just—"

"I don't want to hear a fucking word! You rotten, back-stabbing, piece of shit! You come any closer and I swear, I will fucking kill you!"

Left with no alternatives, he simply stood there while Renee stormed off, and got into the taxi. The driver was polite enough to just ask her "Where to?" instead of commenting on the situation. She told him to head for the police station and he obliged, not saying a word the entire way while she sat in there, wallowing in her own despair.

***

When she'd come to, it was in a hospital bed, a nurse watching over her while she jotted down notes on a clipboard. Once she noticed Chavez had come to, she alerted both the doctor and Jackson Hyde, her partner. The doctor explained how lucky she'd been that someone had treated her wounds, otherwise, she'd be looking at permanent desk duty. When he prescribed her routine over the following weeks, she listened. She'd been insubordinate enough for one lifetime, maybe two.

When the doc left them alone, Hyde lightly chastised her for going alone when she could have been killed. She apologized once more and offered him a chance to get a new partner; one that he could trust with his life. She knew that she'd proven to be undependable these last three days and nights. One of these days, she talk to someone about her ex-husband, and maybe start down the path to re-learning the meaning of trust. But Hyde was having none of it.

"You can't get rid of me that easily, partner," he told her. With the tiniest of blushes, and a few tears that were quickly blinked away, she nodded. Over the course of several days, she was visited by a myriad of people; co-workers, Maurice LeBlanc, members of the church where Michael Strauss had preached. All the while, she found herself searching each new face for a boy in a skull mask. During her time in the hospital, not once did Zero Ozawa visit her, and it bothered her more than she would have liked to admit.

After all, she still had questions, and he was the only one around who could provide answers (LeBlanc didn't want to get into trouble with other *Mononoke* that were here in New Orleans). Not to mention she wanted to thank him for saving her life— *again*—though she hoped he'd be in more polite spirits. She still couldn't get keep the sight of those silver eyes out of her head whenever she thought of him. It was like he'd been a completely different person.

When Captain Braddock finally garnered enough time to come visit her, she asked him about the fate of Detective Marcus O'Mara.

"He's been suspended pending an investigation by Internal Affairs," he sighed. "Don't be surprised if one of the rats comes looking for your statement, Chavez. I know what he did was wrong, and completely against everything we stand for as cops, but I can't help feeling sorry for him. I know what it's like when you just want to set your kid on the right path and nothing going according to plan. It's like there's some force out there that just loves making people's lives miserable."

If you only knew, sir, she had thought with a sympathetic smile.

She'd been released a few days before Halloween and decided to do some shopping, buying up a lot candy and asking Kira Massey to help decorate the house. When they were through, her unassuming home had become a haunted house. And on the night of All Hallows' Eve, she'd entertained a number of trick-or-treaters in her which costume. After three days of sadness, anger, and loss, it felt nice to be able to celebrate something. After all, what was Good Ol' Nawlins if not a city of celebration?

When it was late in the evening, and most of her candy had been given away, save for a few mini-chocolate bars and fruit-flavored gummies, she'd heard a gentle rapping on her door. Opening the door, she saw the last person she expected, dressed as a Ghostbuster of all people. His kind blue eyes glowed as he smiled at her, wielding a fake proton pack, "Trick or treat!"

Whereas any other night, she would have groaned, she laughed, inviting him inside, "I was beginning to think you'd skipped town."

"Still after my blood?"

"Not especially, but you've been on my mind lately."

"I like the sound of that."

"What happened to you? One minute, you're barely able to move, the next, you take out the contractor, burn a house down, and take off without a word."

He blinked at her, expression blank, "I don't know what you're talking about. The last thing I remember was blacking out from the pain of being shot—I'm feeling much better, thanks for asking. Next thing I know, I wake up in some hospital and hear on the news that José killed himself. Which, of course, is the furthest thing from the truth, but I've realized it's much too soon for the worlds of human and spirit to intermingle."

"Then why are you sticking around?" Renee asked. "You pretty much saved the day, whether you remember it or not, isn't this the part where you ride off into the sunset? Or disappear into the night?"

"You watch too many movies," he chuckled. "No, I'm afraid my tenure here is far from over. There's a lead I'm following. Hopefully, it'll pan out this time."

She wondered for a moment what this "lead" could possibly be. She flashed back to the contractor's words, the revelation that it'd only been fulfilling his end of a deal itself. Could whoever it have been working for have anything to do with this?

"And where will you be staying? I get the feeling you're no longer welcome at the church."

"A motel currently provides space for me to rest," he sighed. "I can't say I blame them. I did drag Michael into this mess I wish there was a way to make it up to them, but I doubt they'll ever forgive me. Especially Alexis; she had feelings for him, you know."

"But she couldn't do anything about it," Renee nodded. "A scandal like that would have ruined Strauss's standing. Not to mention if anything had happened around the time of his death, it wouldn't have helped in the least. But if she really cared about him, then she might practice some forgiveness one day."

"In a perfect world," he smiled fondly at her.

182

"Zero," she bit her lip. "If you need a place to stay . . ."

"I couldn't impose," he waved it off. "Besides, what would people say, you letting a teenager live in your house?"

"I don't care what other people say," she stated firmly. "You saved my life and I repay my debts. Besides, it's not like I'm offering you free room and board. You're old enough to start working, so I expect you to pay rent. And when neither of us is working, I want you train me."

"Train you?" he repeated incredulously.

"Not that I don't appreciate you saving me, or giving me back-up," she assured, "I've just never been the 'damsel in distress' type. I want be able to watch my own back in case I'm out there by myself, which'll probably be a lot since I don't intend on letting you interfere with police work. I don't want something like this happening again, so if I can learn how to prevent it, I'll do whatever it takes."

He searched her eyes, seeing her resolve, clear as day, and smiled, leaning back in the chair and wondering how he got himself into these situations. Part of him argued against this, citing her inexperience as being a liability. Another part of him reasoned that the only way to shrug off inexperience was to see battle up close. Still, he feared for her safety; he had enough deaths on his conscious, he didn't know if he could handle anymore. But she wouldn't give up and would seek answers with or without him, so it was a moot point.

"This is a really nice place," he said in lieu of an actual answer. His message got across just fine, anyway. Renee grinned at him and poured some Coke for them both.

"I do believe this is the start of a beautiful... 'friendship.'"

"You really enjoy your classics, don't you, Detective?"

"Renee," she corrected. "Renee Chavez."

"A much more sensible name," he replied cheekily.

"Since we've all but signed a contract," she stood and rounded the table. "There's still one thing left. Paying you back for the other night." She cracked her knuckles; Zero gulped down the soda, burning his throat. Drawing back a fist, Renee grinned when she saw his eyes close in response, waiting for her punch to connect. Instead, she pulled his mask down and kissed his cheek, eliciting a surprised blush from the boy. She smirked triumphantly as he resembled more a teen than he since she met him.

Detective Renee Chavez knew that this was a leap of faith, taking in an almost-stranger with a penchant for wearing skull masks and wielding weapons. It was far more concerning when you considered she knew nothing of his past, or how just how he became the "last of the Ozawa." And why he was even here and what—or who—he was looking for was cause for suspicion. Zero Ozawa was sure to have many secrets hidden away behind more than just a mask, but from what she'd seen, he was someone she could trust. He was someone she needed close by for when the rulebook of reality was thrown out the window.

When things got weird, even by New Orleans standards, she knew she would have to call upon the knowledge he possessed and the lessons he would teach her. But for now, none of that mattered; all Renee knew was one thing; when she came home from work, it would no longer be to an empty household. As strange as he was, Zero would be there to welcome her with a smile, and maybe even help her get past the issues she was having trusting others the way she had trusted Ricardo, who seemed to want back in her life for whatever reason. It was a little much, sure, but hey, a girl was allowed to dream, wasn't she?

With that in mind, she held up her glass and smiled earnestly at Zero, proudly declaring, "Welcome to Nawlins."

Table of Contents

Made in the USA
Coppell, TX
21 April 2022